1

At Blueberry Ridge

Gloria Talley, Virginia Talley, Grace Rapavi

Talley Publishing - Michigan

At Blueberry Ridge

First Edition

Copyright © 2016 Talley Publishing

www.talleypublishing.com

Cover Art drawn by Virginia Talley

Contents:

Chapter One: The Beginning

The air was stuffy and hot. Ann longed to get out of the car. They had been driving for over an hour. Ann looked at her little brown terrier on the seat beside her. She was scratching her ear. Ann's feet felt cramped; her sneakers were way too tight. She leaned up close to the driver's seat, since the radio was blaring, and asked, "Mom, how much longer will it be?" Her mother turned down the radio, just a little.

"We'll be there in about half an hour," she replied. Ann leaned back against her seat.

"Huh," she sighed.

Ann's aunt and uncle had invited her to come spend a couple weeks of the summer with them. It sounded fun, but Ann was a little nervous. Her parents wouldn't be with her, and she didn't know her aunt and uncle hardly at all. It'd been nine years ago she'd seen them last, and she had been only two. Her aunt and uncle owned a nice, large farm with chickens, cows, goats, pigs, and horses.

Ann pulled a book out of her backpack. She opened it, but couldn't concentrate on it. It wasn't interesting. She closed the book with a *snap*. "You hungry, honey?" her mother asked, holding out a bacon snack stick.

"No, thanks."

"Aw, come on. These are your favorites."

"I'm not hungry."

"Is something the matter?"

"Just car sick," Ann said.

"Don't worry, we'll be there in fifteen minutes."

Looking out her open window, Ann could see a lot of land. It stretched for miles. There were some cows with black and white spots. They bent their heads to eat the grass.

"Here we are." Ann's mother pulled into a paved driveway. Ann unbuckled and jumped out of the car. Her terrier jumped out too. Ann opened the car trunk and grabbed her suitcase. She shut the door.

"Goodbye! Have fun," her mother said.

"Wait, aren't you coming in with me?"

"I have to go pick up Danny from softball."

"Why can't Dad?" Ann inquired.

"Your Dad has to go to a meeting for work. Be a good girl and don't forget to write."

"I won't!" called Ann as her mother pulled out of the driveway. Ann waved until her mother was out of sight. Ann took a deep breath and started up the little path to a small but cozy looking house. It was painted the blue of a robin's egg. The shingles on the roof were pine green. Ginger, Ann's terrier, kept running up the path barking and then darting back. She yapped at Ann impatiently for her to hurry up.

"Just a minute, Ginger, this suitcase is heavy." Yes, it was *very* heavy. Ann's hands were red and sticky with sweat.

Just then, the door to the cute little house opened. Out stepped a boy, a few years older than Ann. He was very handsome with dark brown hair, brown eyes, and tanned skin.

"Hi," he grinned, showing a pair of straight, white teeth.

"Hi," Ann said.

"So you're my cousin who's going to stay for some of the summer?"

"Yep."

"That suitcase sure looks heavy, could I carry it for you?"

"Thanks."

Ann handed him the suitcase. As they walked to the house he said, "My name's Dick, what's yours?"

7

"Ann."

"That's a pretty name."

Ann smiled. She felt kind of nervous. They had reached the house. Dick opened the door. They stepped into a tidy, neat kitchen where the aroma of chicken baking in the oven filled the air. "You can put your shoes over here on this mat," Dick told her. Ann neatly placed her shoes on a black mat off to the side.

Dick said, "I like your dog. What's her name?"

"Ginger."

"Cool." Dick bent down and patted Ginger's head. "How you doing, Ginger?" Ginger responded by licking his hand. "I'd like you to meet my mother. Right now, Dad's with my sister Pam tending to the horses."

"Okay." They started across the floor but Ann found it rather slippery in her socks and she fell. "Ow!" she cried out.

"Are you okay?"

"Yeah."

"Sorry, I forgot to warn you. Mom just cleaned the floor. It's still kind of wet." Dick held out his hand. Ann grabbed it and with a strong arm Dick pulled Ann to her feet.

In the dining room, a short stout woman was setting the table. "She's here, Mom," Dick announced. The woman whirled around. She looked Ann up and down.

"You've changed quite a lot. You use to be shorter than my waist and now I believe you're taller than me. You're quite skinny, but have no fear, we'll fatten you up in no time. Ann, dear, it'll be dinner time soon but Dick will show you to your room," her aunt chattered on. "Make yourself at home."

"Thank you, ma'am."

"Don't ma'am me. It ain't the old days no more. You can call me Aunt Jane, just like a niece should."

"Yes, Aunt Jane."

Dick led the way to where Ann's room was to be. "What do you think of her?" asked Dick.

"She's nice," Ann said.

"Well, here you are. Just call if you need something." He winked and left.

"He sure is a friendly boy," Ann thought. "I think we'll get along just fine." She opened the door to the guest room.

Ann was absolutely charmed with her room. There was a soft bed covered with a fresh white sheet. The walls were purple-pink and the floor shone brightly. An oak dresser faced the bed on the opposite wall. A colorful rug lay on the floor by the bed. A cute little window overlooked the yard.

Ann flew to the window. Outside, she could see the barn and lazy pigs rolling in the mud inside a pen. The sky was bright blue and the grass was fresh green. Ann loved the beautiful scenery. Somebody knocked on Ann's door. Ann opened it.

"Supper's ready," said Aunt Jane.

"Okay." Ann followed her aunt back to the dining room.

A girl of seventeen or eighteen was seated next to Dick. She looked quite like him and was very pretty. Her brown hair fell about her face and her brown eyes sparkled with excitement. A tall husky man sat at one end of the table. He had a scruffy beard, grayish hair, and glasses.

Aunt Jane sat at the end of the table opposite Ann's uncle. Ann took a seat across from Dick's sister. The food before her looked delicious: crispy chicken, mashed potatoes, and corn on the cob. Uncle Nick led them in grace. They ended with a resounding "Amen."

Ann dug into her mashed potatoes. They were perfect.

Dick's sister introduced herself. "Hi Ann, I don't know if you remember me at all. My name is Pam. I was eight when you were here last. I'm sure we'll have lots of fun together."

Ann smiled. "I hope so," she said.

9

"Are you into animals much?" asked Pam.

"Um, yes. Have you seen my terrier Ginger?" Ann asked as she cut off a piece of chicken.

"Oh, yes. She's very cute."

"Mmm… this is delicious," Ann complemented.

"Glad you like it," said Aunt Jane.

"Would you like to see my horse after dinner? She's a beauty," Pam asked Ann.

"Um…" Ann tried to think of an excuse, "No, I'm rather tired. I'd like to get to bed early. Maybe tomorrow."

"Okay," Pam said. Ann didn't really want to see Pam's horse. She and horses didn't go well together. Why, a horse could crush her and kill her if it willed. She could remember the time when she was only five and a horse had stepped on her foot. She remembered how badly it had hurt.

She could also remember when she was seven; how she'd been on a trail ride, and had lost control of her horse and it had run off from the guide. How scared she had been! Ann felt full; she looked down at her plate. Most of her chicken was still there, she'd only taken a few bites of corn, and her mashed potatoes were gone. "I'm not really hungry anymore," Ann said aloud.

"Saints alive! Not hungry, mashed potatoes won't fill you up. But if that's how you feel, your dinner will be in the fridge when you are hungry." Aunt Jane dismissed her.

Ann washed up in the bathroom. Next, she climbed upstairs to her room. She started unpacking. She folded her clothes and stacked them in the dresser. This was quite a time-consuming process, since she had quite a lot of clothes. Ann wasn't actually tired, so she went downstairs to see what was going on. In the dining room, Dick and his father were playing chess.

"Hi," said Dick, "I just about got Dad beat."

"Nope," said Uncle Nicholas. "Check!"

"Huh," sighed Dick, "I didn't expect you to make *that* move."

"Where's Aunt Jane?" Ann asked.

"She's in the living room watching something on TV," said Dick.

Ann found the living room. Aunt Jane was watching something that looked like an exercise video.

"Hi Ann, want to follow along with me? It gives you a good workout."

"All right!" agreed Ann,

"Okay, first let's get warmed up," the woman on TV said. "Stretch your arms over your head, now bend down to reach your toes. Next let's try some jumping jacks: one, two, three, four..."

Ann and Aunt Jane followed the exercises: pushups, sit-ups, running in place, leg lifts, arm circles, and more. When it was over they were both exhausted. Aunt Jane turned off the TV. "That's how I like to watch television," Aunt Jane said, "You don't just sit there and be lazy. Besides, it's fun."

Ann nodded. "Well, I'm going to bed now. It's almost nine, I'll see you in the morning."

"Okay."

Ann gave her Aunt a big hug and said goodnight. She wandered back to the dining room.

"I just beat dad at chess," chuckled Dick.

"Beat! You barely beat me. I had you until you got that promotion," Uncle Nicholas retorted.

"Well, still, it's the first time I ever beat you," Dick said.

"It's also the last time," grumbled his father, setting up the chessboard to play again.

"I'm going to sleep, see you in the morning. If you see Pam, say goodnight to her for me," Ann told them.

"Sweet dreams," Uncle Nick said.

"Goodnight," said Dick.

Ann entered her bedroom. She got dressed into her pajamas and brushed her teeth. She looked in the mirror while she combed her wavy light brown hair; it fell just past her shoulders. Her blue eyes stared into the clear glass. Ann smiled. She put the brush away. Ann climbed into bed. It had been fun so far, and she knew it was just the beginning of her adventures at Blueberry Ridge.

Chapter Two: Trouble at Breakfast

Ann woke to Aunt Jane's voice calling her from outside the bedroom door.

"Ann, don't you want to get up? It's six o'clock already!"

Ann turned over in her bed. There wasn't much light in the room, because the curtain was closed. Ann felt very warm and dreamy.

Finally, she rolled out of bed and replied, "I'll be right down!"

"Ok! We have lots of fun things planned for today. Pam wants to take you riding…" Ann froze where she was.

Riding? She didn't even hear the rest of what Aunt Jane was saying. *Well, how I am going to get out of this?* Ann thought, getting dressed into some jeans and a pink T-shirt. She didn't want to upset Pam, or Aunt Jane. But she *really* didn't like horses.

Going downstairs, Ann heard Dick talking excitedly, "...yeah, we can show her that fort that you and me made when we were little."

"She might like it. It was pretty cool back then, although it's a bit childish for us now," replied Pam.

Ann heard the clatter of dishes and knew that they must be eating. She entered the kitchen.

"Good morning, sleepy head!" Dick greeted her cheerfully.

"Good morning. It's not all that late," Ann countered.

"I know, I'm just teasing," Dick laughed. Ann thought his laugh was very nice. It made her want to laugh too, but she just smiled.

"You have ridden before, I presume?" Aunt Jane asked, as she placed a plate of hot cinnamon buns before Ann. "Help yourself," she added.

"Uh, yes I have. Quite a while ago," Ann replied quickly, as she took a bun. Hoping to change the topic, Ann said, "Did you make these yourself?" She took a bite. It was very buttery and warm. It was delicious.

"No, actually Pam made them. She's a very good cook, unlike her mother." Aunt Jane poked fun at herself.

"They *are* very good." Ann said to Pam.

"I'm glad you like them!" Pam answered.

Yet Ann did not get her wish; they continued to talk about the dreaded subject.

"Ann, you can ride my horse, Ivy. He is very friendly. He is light brown, with white mane and tail. I think you'll like him."

Ann did not care what color the horse was. She didn't want to ride any horse. And that was a fact. Ann looked down at her plate.

"Is something the matter?" Aunt Jane looked concerned. Ann's first reaction was to say no, but thinking better of it, she answered, "Well, I don't know. It's just that I'd rather not ride the horses today."

As soon as Ann said this, she wished she had left out the 'today' part of her sentence.

"Maybe we will ride tomorrow then, or you might feel like it later," Pam answered.

Great, thought Ann, *now I'll have to keep on dreading it.*

"Maybe you would like to just look at the horses," invited Dick.

Ann started to get upset. "No, I would not! I'm sick of talking about horses!" she cried, as she shoved back her plate, and got

14

out of her chair. She ran to the back door and raced outside, tears rolling down her cheeks.

Ann raced across the yard. She heard Ginger barking happily. She scampered up next to her. *Not now, Ginger,* Ann thought as she sobbed. She just wanted to be alone, by herself, with her own thoughts. Ann was so mad she didn't even think about where she was going. She flew to the red barn and threw open the door. It was dim and lonely. Ann sat down on a wooden stool and cried and cried, not even thinking about where she was.

Oh, my summer was going to be so wonderful, now it's all ruined! Nobody even cares about me, they just care about horses! Horses, horses, horses! Ann breathed ragged short breaths, as her thoughts raced inside her. Suddenly Ann stopped crying. She thought she heard someone moving around in the barn, but it was hard to tell where. She stood up and began to walk as she looked about.

Straw and hay bits were scattered along the ground. Ann could see bales of hay stacked high. There was food bags, halters, reins, and saddles around the barn. Ann heard the noise again. Then she turned around to find herself face to face with a horse! Ann stumbled back in shock. Then she told herself, *Why of course there's a horse! It is a barn after all.* And the horse was very pretty, even Ann had to admit.

The creamy white forelock ran past his deep black eyes. The horse pushed his big head over the fence in the stall and nudged Ann's shoulder. Ann was surprised to feel how soft his muzzle was. The horse began to lick Ann's bare arm with his big tongue. Ann pulled her arm away, but it did remind her of something a puppy would do. Perhaps, just perhaps, the horse was okay; but Ann wasn't sure. Ann slowly held out her hand and patted the horse's forehead.

The horse seemed to enjoy it. Ann grew bolder and brushed the forelock out of the horses eyes. She was surprised to see a small white patch. Ann vaguely remembered her mother telling her that a spot like that was called a star. Ann stepped back and looked at the horse. *I guess I was acting pretty stupid,* she thought, *They all must think I'm crazy.* Just then Ann realized something. If anyone were to find her here, it would look pretty ridiculous!

To be crying about not liking horses and then run into the barn where the horses were! No, Ann had to get out, and fast; before she was misunderstood. But it was too late. Ann could hear the barn door creaking open. Ann looked around wildly. She stole across the floor, and hid behind the hay bales. The scratchy hay brushed against Ann's face. Her breathing seemed too loud. Soon the door was open all the way.

Ann heard Dick's voice, "Ann, are you here? Where are you? We're all worried about you. We didn't know. I'm sorry." There was a short pause. "Come on, we've been looking for you. I didn't think you'd be in here, but we've looked almost everywhere, except for the trails." Ann felt sorry for him to have to look for her, but should she come out? Or not? Which would win, her conscience or her pride? Ann couldn't make up her mind. Struggling with her decision, she finally broke free. Ann jumped out of her hiding spot.

"Here I am," she blurted, turning red in the face.

Dick seemed relieved and quickly walked over to Ann. "I'm really sorry about saying what I said. I didn't mean to be rude."

Ann was surprised. "I was the one being rude," she replied shyly, "I don't know what's wrong with me."

"I do," grinned Dick.

"What do you mean?"

"I know," said Dick, folding his arms, "I didn't like horses either, that is, until last year…" he trailed off.

"You? How could you not like horses? Haven't you had horses all your life?" Ann asked, amazed.

"I don't know, I just thought they were a lot of work till now."

"What made you change your mind?" Now Ann was curious.

"Ivy, that's what made me change my mind. You should see him. He's wonderful." Dick praised his horse.

"I already have," Ann found herself saying.

Dick didn't seem to have heard her. He walked towards Ivy's stall. Ivy shook his creamy mane and pawed the ground impatiently.

"It's okay, boy," Dick said softly, stroking the smooth neck. "See," he said barely above a whisper. Ivy blinked and put his head against Dick.

Ann didn't know what to say or what to do. She wanted to be Dick's friend and maybe she could learn to like horses after all, but could she ride one?

After a while, Dick told Ann, "Come on, let's go." He walked out of the barn and Ann followed. Yet Dick didn't go back to the house like Ann had expected. It looked like he were about to say something when Pam hurried over,

"Oh, there you are!" she cried, "Mom, Pop! I found them!"

Aunt Jane and Uncle Nick soon appeared. Ann expected them to ask where she'd been, but they didn't.

Aunt Jane just said, "It's not nice manners to keep your pretty cousin all to yourself, Dick. You have to share her with the rest of us." Dick opened his mouth to say something and then shut it after one look from his father.

"Yes, mom," he replied.

"Perhaps," said Pam, "we should all like to take a walk?"

"That's a fine idea," said Aunt Jane, always eager to get some exercise. So the five of them started down the trail that ran through the woods in the back of the yard.

"We have twenty acres of land," remarked Uncle Nick.

"That is a lot," replied Ann, not knowing what else to say. There was silence for a while, but Ann did not mind. The trail was beautiful. Lots of chirping American Goldfinches, Chickadees, Cedar Waxwings, and other little birds. The trees were very leafy, and occasionally Ann saw a squirrel. The morning dew sparkled on the grass, and buttercups were sprinkled alongside the path. The air was cool and refreshing.

Presently, they came to a fork in the trail. "Let's go left," announced Uncle Nick.

"Is left the right one?" joked Dick.

"In this case, yes. The left path leads to the right path, anyhow," Pam told Ann.

"Oh," said Ann. So they began down the left path. Finally someone spoke. This time, it was Aunt Jane.

She said, "Ann, have you ever done any quilting?"

"No."

"Would you like to learn?"

Ann said she did, although she wasn't so sure.

"I have lots of pretty cloth. When you go home, you'll have a nice pretty quilt for your bed. I'm sure your mom will be quite proud of you."

At that moment, Ann secretly promised herself that she would try hard to make a quilt. Not just to impress Aunt Jane, but for her own sake at determination. As they turned back to the house, Pam asked Ann, "Would you like to see our goats? We have four girls, and two boys. We also have a baby goat that was born not very long ago."

"Sure, sounds fun," Ann replied. She couldn't wait to see the baby goat! They came out of the woods and neared the pen with the goats. All of a sudden, there came a terrible squawking and almost screaming from the chicken coop!

"Whatever is going on?" Ann asked,

"I don't know! Something must be in the coop!" Pam cried, as they rushed towards the chicken coop.

Chapter Three: The Forgotten Past

They saw something from the corner of their eyes...

"What is it?" questioned Ann, worried it would bring down the family's mood. Pam opened the small gate that led to where the chickens were trying to scramble about. Feathers fell and covered the dark dirt; they brushed against the tough wired fence. "A dog!" Ann exclaimed, presenting the obvious.

"Not just any dog... the neighbor's dog!" Pam exclaimed. There was a hole in the fence, and the mangy animal was trying to catch a chicken, more like kill the chicken.

The family finally caught the vicious dog before it could eat the chickens.

"Where is the closest neighbor?" Ann wondered, looking far and seeing no neighbors but only fields.

"There are some only a couple miles west. This dog comes around occasionally. We have to talk to them about it, and fix that hole!" Pam cried enthusiastically.

Another chore added to Ann's summer, would she be only working and riding? The dog started to head towards the direction of its home.

Pam thanked her cousin for helping her catch the dog. The cows were milked and now grazed in the pastures. The horses bathed in the sun. Pam went to clean the stalls of the horses, something Ann would start doing tomorrow. "Watch and learn!" was how Aunt Jane described it.

Dick approached Ann, hoping to gently bring up the horse topic. "I saw you help Pam catch the dog. I must say, you're a natural!"

"Thanks, I'm glad we got to him first!" A smile traced her beaming face.

"What happened? I mean, with you and the horses before?"

"My experiences with horses are not the best. I got stepped on by one when I was five, and then got practically abandoned by another when I was seven."

Dick stood there, surprised as he realized the pain she had went through. Dick thought to himself. *Maybe, just maybe, Ivy could change her mind.* Ann first had to trust him, then maybe she would trust horses. They both went back into the barn. Ivy and some other horses stood in their stalls. They were either eating their hay, or waiting to be groomed and petted.

Ann slowly crept towards Ivy. Dick noticed her hesitation, while remembering what happened when she was a little girl.

"This is Ivy," he said, "he doesn't bite or nip. And better yet, he doesn't step on people's toes."

Ann slowly but surely reached her hand over the stall door. The beautiful horse leaned forward, wanting to meet another friend. Dick started petting Ivy, hoping his cousin would follow along and forget her past.

"Want to groom him?" Dick asked, unlatching the stall door.

"Only if you stay right here with me!" announced Ann, not wanting any one-on-one time with a horse anywhere in the near future.

"I will. Here, I'll teach you. It's easy!" Dick grabbed the grooming tools. Ann took a few steps back. Dick led Ivy into the middle aisle so there would be more room to groom him. Ann was getting nervous, was she actually doing this?

"Okay, now we are just going to start with this brush here. He's only a little dusty after our last trail ride." Dick demonstrated. Ann cautiously followed, still afraid. As memories rushed in she tried to remember that this was a different horse. It was a friendly horse for that matter, and she was much older now, with an excellent teacher to guide her.

"Like this?" she asked, hoping at least she was starting to get the hang of it.

"Yep, just make sure not to brush too hard or too soft. Somewhere in between is usually best."

Ann smiled in appreciation at Dick's helpful advice.

Dick started a conversation. "Later today, we were planning on picking some blueberries. They seem to be early this year. Do you like berries?"

"Yes! Especially blueberries. That sounds nice, a little rest from grooming horses," replied Ann, glad to join in another family-like activity.

"Dick! Ann!" a voice shouted from the front porch. "Come on in, time for lunch!" Aunt Jane went back inside, to put the food on the table.

"Already?" Ann thought out loud. All that hard work flew by fast and made her very hungry.

"Let's put these away, then." Dick gently took the brush and comb from his cousin and put them in the grooming box.

"Thanks for teaching me. I guess I'm still getting used to all of this kind of stuff."

"You're doing great! You'll get the hang of it." His encouraging statement helped Ann realize how horses aren't what she had pictured them as before. After putting Ivy back and the tools away, Dick led Ann out of the barn and latched the door.

Heading towards the house, they saw someone pull into the rocky-dirt driveway. "Hmm… wonder who that could be," Dick said, walking faster.

"Do you normally have visitors?" Ann asked curiously.

"Not much, except for private piano lessons and some occasional social gatherings."

A man stepped out of the old-looking car. Who could it be? After knocking on the wooden door, he was let in by Aunt Jane. Dick and Ann waited for him to leave. It only took about five minutes, and the man was gone. Then they went in through the back door.

"Who was that guy?" Dick asked.

"Yeah, and why was he here?" followed Ann.

They both sat down. Pam pointed to the paper that was on the counter. "He left this."

Dick began to read it. "Looks like a competition. A horse competition. It's coming up in a couple Saturdays."

Ann leaned over to look at it. "Are you going to enter?"

"You bet I will!" Dick replied. He hoped Ann would too. Maybe this competition was just what Ann needed to get her mind off things.

"You could help me train and get ready, Ann," Dick gently elbowed his cousin, hoping she would compete in the competition too. "There are a few different competitions. There's one for the best looking horse, then there is jumping, and racing."

"Ivy could win all three..." Ann thought out loud. He was definitely the handsomest!

"Have you ever entered a competition before?" Ann then asked.

"Some. But none as big as this!" Dick replied, putting the piece of paper down.

Then they said grace and started eating. There was chicken and ham sandwiches with fruit and lemonade.

"After we go blueberry picking, we'll have enough berries to make pies, and muffins, and cakes! And some to just eat!" Aunt Jane seemed a little too excited just to pick berries. But Ann was also excited to go. Plus pies, cakes, and muffins sounded good to her. After finishing lunch, Ann helped clean up. The others got ready to go berry-picking.

Ann still wasn't real sure about the horse competition. She was trying not to think about what actually could go wrong. They would start training tomorrow. She would be prepared. And she did know one thing: she was not going to let her past experiences get the better of her!

Chapter Four: Blueberry Ridge

They all five got their pails for picking blueberries and started off.

"It's not very far to the blueberry patch. It's just up the road," Pam told Ann.

"Great." Ann smiled, but she had a different thought on her mind. "So, Dick, if I did enter the competition..." Ann paused.

"Yes?" Dick encouraged.

"Well, you'd be entering Ivy. Who could I enter?"

"Oh," said Dick, "We have a lot of nice horses. Why don't you pick one out after berry picking? You can test them out and see which one you like."

"Okay."

Ann stopped. In front of them was a field of great big luscious blueberries. They made Ann's mouth water at the very sight. There was a dirt path through the bushes so they wouldn't have to be trampled on. Ann began picking them and dropping them in her pail. She was surprised at the rapid rate that her pail was filling with the delicious fruit. She glanced over at Dick. He was popping far more into his mouth than his pail. Ann realized she hadn't even tried a single berry. She tried a great big juicy berry.

"Mmm..." said Ann. The taste was scrumptiously good. She continued picking berries, eating a few as she worked. Ann stood up. Her back ached from bending over.

"How's the picking going?" Uncle Nick inquired.

"Wonderful, my pail is almost full," Ann replied.

"Good," said Uncle Nick, "I filled two pails. Now I'm heading back home."

"Okay, see you in a little while," said Ann.

Soon Pam, Ann, Aunt Jane, and Dick's pails were also full. They started back home.

"Berry picking sure is hard work," said Ann.

"But it's worth it," said Dick munching on another plump berry.

"You bet," said Ann.

"Mom," Pam said to Aunt Jane, "that neighbor's dog is getting to be a real problem. Today, he was at the chicken's again."

"Oh, was he now?" Aunt Jane sounded annoyed.

"I think we ought to talk to the owner about it," said Pam.

"I'll ask your father to," Aunt Jane replied.

They approached the house. Ginger raced up to Ann, yapping excitedly. She put her paws up on Ann. Whimpering, she tried to stick her head in Ann's blueberry pail, hoping to eat some herself.

"Down, Ginger," Ann commanded firmly. Ginger obeyed and ran to the door of the house.

They all went inside and placed their pails on the table next to Uncle Nick's. Uncle Nick was reading about the horse competition.

"Do you think we can go?" Dick pleaded.

"I don't see why not," his father said.

"And I'd like to help Ann so she can enter too."

"Oh?" Uncle Nick looked up from the paper.

Ann felt nervous under his cool glance.

Suddenly there came a crashing sound from the kitchen. Ann jumped up from the couch and rushed to the kitchen. Ginger was gobbling up a pail of blueberries she had managed to pull off the table.

"Ginger!" Ann scolded. Ginger looked up.

"No worry, we've still got five pails," said Aunt Jane, upon entering the kitchen. Pam put the rest of the blueberries in the fridge.

"We can make some muffins or something later," Pam said to Ann, "Do you want to see the goats now? We never really got a chance earlier."

"Sure!" Ann was glad nobody was really bothered about Ginger.

The cousins went to the pen.

The baby goat frolicked about on its legs. He was so cute! Pam and Ann entered the pen. Ann knelt down and pet the baby goat. His ears were soft and tender and his fur was soft and warm. The baby goat ran to its mother. The little goat bent down on its knees and drank her warm milk. Ann was charmed. "Oh, he's absolutely darling!" she exclaimed.

The male goats had horns, whereas the females did not have horns nearly as big. One goat bent to munch a clump of grass.

"Hey Ann," Dick greeted, approaching her.

"Yeah?" Ann did not take her eyes off the baby goat.

"Would you like to come look at the horses now?" Dick asked. Ann hesitated. She was still a bit afraid of horses. It was only this morning she had been tired of people talking about them. She dearly loved the goats so much she felt that she could watch the baby forever. But she was feeling more comfortable with horses, and she actually did want to see them...

"Sure," Ann pulled her eyes off the baby goat. She could always come see him later.

"You don't have to if you want to stay with the goats," Dick did not want to force her.

"Nah," said Ann.

"I've been trying to show Ann that horses aren't so bad. She just had a bad experience a long time ago," Dick explained to Pam.

In the barn besides Ivy, there was a beautiful red-brown horse with a slightly darker mane and tail. His left hind leg had a white stocking.

"He's very handsome," Ann said studying the strong stallion, "What's his name?"

"Daylight," said Dick.

The next stall contained a dark brown mare with a slightly tinted red mane and tail. She had a white star just like Ivy's.

Dick introduced the horses. "This is Autumn." Ann also met Lilac, a black mare. Crystal and Jewel, Dick told Ann, were twin brother and sister. They were whitish-grayish.

"They're all so beautiful," Ann gasped. Dick had finished giving his tour.

"Would you like to take one out and lead it?" asked Dick. Ann stepped back.

"Well, I..."

"Come on, they won't hurt you," Dick reassured her.

"Well, alright." Ann took a while choosing one. Ivy, by far, was the handsomest, but he was Dick's horse.

"Autumn," Ann decided at last. She was a very pretty horse and very gentle.

"Okay," Dick grabbed Autumn's halter off a hook. He entered her stall and brought out Autumn. Dick tried to show Ann how the halter fitted on, but Ann didn't really understand. Dick led Autumn out of the barn. Ann began stroking Autumn's mane. The mare sniffed Ann's hand and licked it with her warm wet tongue.

"Here's the rope," said Dick. Ann was a bit frightened. She held the rope in one hand as Dick directed and held the halter under Autumn's chin and led Autumn around a tree.

"Not bad," praised Dick. Ann smiled. Gradually, she was liking horses more. Maybe they weren't that big and scary after all. Ann handed the rope back to Dick. He understood. He didn't want to push her.

"How about some more practice tomorrow?" he asked.

"Sure." Dick put Autumn back into her stall. Ann held out an apple as a treat to the horse. Autumn sniffed it curiously, then crunched it down delightfully. Ann patted Autumn's head.

Inside the house, Aunt Jane was talking to Uncle Nick. "I think you are too much of a Mr. Nice Guy. This is the third time you've had to go over there this week. If my chickens don't lay as many eggs I'll know why. Why don't you just call the police and have the guy pay a fine? There are leash laws you know."

"If it happens again, I'll be sure to call the police," Uncle Nick said. He went outside.

"Where are you going, Dad?" Dick asked.

"To talk to that neighbor."

"Oh," said Dick. Dick and Ann went inside.

"Richard," Aunt Jane got Dick's attention, "Would you fix that hole in the chicken coop?"

"Sure thing, Mom."

"Ann?" Pam asked, "Would you like to come with me to meet some of my friends? They've been begging me to come see their baby bunnies, but I've been so busy."

"Sure! I'd love to come!"

They set out towards Pam's friend's house. "It's about a half mile walk," Pam said.

"What is this street called? I mean, it's beautiful," said Ann looking at the scenery as she walked along.

"Blueberry Ridge. Isn't it a nice street to live on?"

"It certainly is."

A little while later they reached their destination. A large blue house stood in a freshly mown lawn. A girl about Pam's age was watering some daylilies.

"Hi, Layla!" Pam called out.

"Oh, hi!" the girl turned and smiled. Her blond hair fell about her shoulders and her bright pink cheeks shone.

Ann and Pam went over to Layla. "This is my cousin Ann, she'll be staying with us for a couple weeks," Pam explained.

"Hi. Would you like to see our baby bunnies? We just started selling them yesterday and we already sold two of them. In fact, Taylor's over there right now. I'll meet you over there." Layla pointed towards the hutch.

The cousins walked to the hutch. A young girl of twelve held a rabbit. She looked very much like her sister. "Hi Pam," she said.

"Hi, Taylor," Pam said and introduced Ann.

"How do you like your stay with Pam so far?" Taylor inquired.

"It's been very fun."

"This is Maple," Taylor showed them the dark brown rabbit she held, "He's the father of all the babies."

Ann peered into the hutch. "Oh, they're so cute!" she exclaimed. There were four babies, and their brown and white mother. Two of the babies were dark brown, one was white with light brown patches, and the other was all white. They wiggled their noses. Ann was so absorbed in the rabbits she didn't even hear Pam and her friends talking.

"How much do they cost?" Ann asked suddenly.

"Twelve dollars," replied Taylor, "do you want one?"

"Yes, but I don't know what my parents would say..."

"You can come back later when you know for sure," said Layla.

30

"But don't wait too long, they might be all gone," added Taylor.

"Well," said Pam, "I think we should be getting back home for dinner."

"Ok," Ann took her hand off the rabbit's soft fur.

Arriving home, the cousins sat down to Aunt Jane's spaghetti. After supper Ann decide to write a letter to her parents. After all, she had to keep her promise. She put pencil to paper and began:

Dear Mom and Dad and Danny too,

     I hope you all are well. I've been having quite an exciting time. Aunt Jane and Uncle Nick are very kind, and I've made two of the best friends any girl could wish for, my cousins Pam and Dick. I've been thinking, maybe horses aren't so scary. I really quite like them now; it's almost funny. It seems like I've been away so long, though I've only just completed my first day here at Blueberry Ridge. That's what they call the street here, and it's a good name too. We've got six pails of delicious blueberries! (Well, Ginger did eat one whole pail). This might seem strange to ask, but, could I have a pet rabbit? Pam's friends are selling them, and well, I'd really like one. They are adorable. I'm looking forward to hearing from you!

Love always,

Ann Melonwood

Ann set her letter aside on a bedside table. She would mail it tomorrow. She clicked off her lamp and climbed into bed to dream of goats, horses, and bunnies, all on Blueberry Ridge.

Chapter Five: Wet, Muddy Excitement

The next day did not prove nice weather. Even from the moment Ann woke up it was dark and rainy. Ann sighed. Somehow, she had looked forward to training with the horses. Ann leaned her forehead on the cold window pane. The world looked gray and gloomy. The barn looked a strange dark red in the rain.

Ann idly tapped her fingers. Her gaze fell to the pastures where the horses would graze in good weather. For now, they were in the barn, dry and safe. At last, Ann slipped out of her nightgown and put on a pair of blue jeans and a purple button up blouse. She combed her hair into three parts and platted it. Finally she went to the kitchen to figure out what was on the menu for breakfast.

On the way down the stairs, Ann smelled a wave of sweetness. Blueberry pancakes! She hurried to greet her cousins and their parents.

"Good morning!" Pam sang out to Ann.

"Good morning," she replied. Pam was pouring small circles of batter onto the grill. Ann looked about. There was nobody else in the room.

"Where is everyone?" Ann asked seating herself at the kitchen table. Pam didn't answer for a moment. "Did you hear me?" Ann inquired.

"Oh, ah... Dick and my mom and Dad went to, ah..." Pam paused trying to figure out the correct word to use.

"Yes?" Ann encouraged.

"Well I am not really supposed to tell," Pam said at last.

"Come on," Ann urged, "You can tell me."

"I really shouldn't tell. Listen, I'll tell you later, or you'll find out later."

"Is it a surprise?" Ann asked.

"Remember, I'm not allowed to say. Do you want a pancake?" Pam changed the subject.

"Sure, they look yummy." Pam scooped up a pancake off the grill with a spatula. She set it down on a plate in front of Ann. Ann forked a piece and bit it.

"Ow!" she exclaimed.

"Oh, Ann. I'm so sorry," Pam apologized, "I forgot to tell you that they're hot!"

"I'm okay. I should have known."

As she waited for the blueberry pancakes to cool, Ann said, "Pam? It's too bad it had to rain. I, well..." Ann paused. She wanted to tell Pam how sorry she was about the incident at breakfast yesterday; but she just didn't know how to begin.

"I'm sorry," she said rather more quickly than she had meant. Pam seemed not to understand.

"About what?"

"About being upset at you guys yesterday," Ann managed to say.

"That's alright. You were just a little nervous and uneasy about being in a new place. We were also just a little too excited to show off our horses."

Pam is so nice, thought Ann.

Just then, Uncle Nick opened the front door. More like he *threw* open the front door. He did not look happy one bit. His dark eyebrows were knit in a frown and he walked swiftly to the kitchen. His clothes were drenched and muddy.

"Pa-" Pam began but Uncle Nick cut her short.

"Pam, never trust mechanics! That motor in the truck isn't working again." He grumbled to himself and then continued

34

saying, "I had to walk three miles to come back here. Dick and your mom are..." he paused a second looking straight at Ann, "Well never mind them. That truck is stuck on the road. Guess I'll call the tow-truck. Get the phone, Pam."

"Yes, Pa." Pam hurriedly got the phone.

"I'm sorry you got so muddy," said Ann.

"I'm alright. Dick and your Aunt are still at the truck waiting. They had to stay with the chickens. We're trading them for ducklings. You want to come with me in the car?"

"Sure!" Ann exclaimed. She was sorry that the truck had broken down, but at least she knew where they were! And ducklings! How Ann loved baby animals!

Ann quickly ate up her pancake and grabbed a second one to take with her.

"Why did you go so early in the morning?" she asked Uncle Nick.

"Only time the people could trade. Anyways, it was going to sort of be a surprise for you. Pam said you'd love the baby ducks."

"Indeed I would!" Ann clapped her hands happily. She skipped to the car.

Meanwhile, Pam had telephoned the tow-truck and stayed home to finish cooking. Uncle Nick still seemed disgusted with the truck breaking down and kept muttering things to himself like, "Can't get a new truck any time soon. They don't make them like they use to. They don't fix 'em like they use to either." Ann couldn't make out whether he was talking to himself or her. It didn't really matter though.

At last, they arrived at the broken-down truck. You would not have known it was broken down though, just by looking at it. The tow-truck arrived shortly and the pickup was towed away to be repaired. Dick and Aunt Jane had moved the chickens to the car.

"Too bad our little surprise is spoiled. You'll have fun enough though," Aunt Jane smiled. Ann smiled back. At least Aunt Jane didn't care to be grumpy about an old truck. One thing was for sure, she didn't show it if she was.

Ann climbed in the car next to Dick in the back seat. She said to him, "Why'd you decide to try ducks?"

"We've had chickens for a while, guess my mom thought we'd try something different. Do you still want to help me train Ivy?"

"It's raining right now, do you think it will clear up? I would like to help, but I don't know what I can do to help."

"I think it will clear up. You can help in lots of ways. I'll need some help setting up the fence for the jumping, someone to time how fast Ivy runs, more grooming, and well...lots of stuff."

"Sounds like a lot of work," Ann replied.

"You bet, but it's worth it. There are prizes and ribbons for the winners."

"Do you think we stand a good chance at winning?"

"No way to tell really, but having fun is the most important part," Dick reminded Ann.

"Right."

The car drove on past large stretches of land in the early gray morning. The rain did not pour, but came down in a steady drizzle.

"Nice day for ducks," laughed Aunt Jane, looking at the weather. The chickens squawked in their small wire cages in the back of the car. "Sure are noisy little things, Ann, aren't they?"

"Sure are. How many are there?"

"Oh, we have twelve chickens."

Twisting around and leaning on the back of her seat, Ann looked at the speckled hens. She counted them just for fun. One two, three... seven, eight. Why, there were only eight!

Ann turned around and called to Aunt Jane, "Why, I just counted and there are only eight!"

"Are you quite sure?"

"Yes, definitely."

"Well, maybe I was wrong. Maybe there are only eight. Dick, you fixed that hole in the fence right?"

"Yes, Mom."

Uncle Nick turned to a back road and stopped at a small farm. Everyone got out. They headed towards a little white house, but before they reached it, a young man came out and greeted them.

"Hi, the ducklings are in the shed. I'll go get them for you." And he was off.

The man brought the ducks and Aunt Jane got the chickens. Soon they were on their way again. Ann didn't have a chance to see the ducklings yet, they were in a covered box. Aunt Jane had said, "Just wait till we get home," and after a peek at them herself to make sure they looked fine they drove back to Blueberry Ridge.

Uncle Nick seemed in better spirits on the way back.

"I just thought of something," he said, "If I sell this car and then maybe we will have enough for a new truck. We don't much use this one except when the other breaks down."

"Now that's thinking," said his wife.

As they pulled into the driveway, the rain let up. Ann jumped out of the car excitedly, yet, alas! She landed in a wet muddy puddle.

"Yuck!" she laughed. Dick and Ann showed Pam the soft yellow ducklings, and watched them play for a while. They were so cute and funny. Soon, though, the ducklings huddled together and closed their bright black eyes and rested their webbed feet. The children ate some pancakes and then Dick said, "Maybe it's time to start training!"

Dick looked excited. It was still rather wet, but they picked their way around the messy puddles to the barn. Aunt Jane and Uncle Nick were inside. Pam unlatched the door and lead the way inside. "If you want, I'll muck a few stalls while you guys get started," offered Pam.

"Thanks!" Ann smiled, glad to get started.

Dick opened Ivy's stall and began fastening the halter and reins, explaining as he went. "Now, I will get the saddle. Hold his halter a sec."

Dick came back with the heavy saddle and the pad that went under the saddle. Putting the pad on and then the saddle, Dick showed Ann how to get ready.

He showed Ann how to adjust the girth. "It's very important to check the girth. If it is too loose the saddle will slide around and you could fall off, but not too tight because it could hurt the horse. Good, that seems right." Next he adjusted the stirrups.

"Alrighty, we are ready to go." Dick took the lead rope and lead Ivy out of the barn. Ann followed.

The horse shook his mane and started to trot. "Whoa, boy. Hold on a minute," Dick tried to stop Ivy. Ivy slowed down a little. "He's probably tired of being in his stall too long. I should have brought him out yesterday." Dick brought Ivy over to some wooden steps so he could get on better. Dick snapped on a helmet.

"Always good to be safe!"

Dick handed Ann a stop watch, and explained how to time him. Then Dick put his foot in the stirrup and swung the other leg over. He gave Ivy a slight kick and steered him to the left away from the steps and walked Ivy to a clearing. Ann came over to watch. "Alright now, Ann, start the watch and stop it after 3 laps around the ring, okay?"

"Okay!" cried Ann. Ann pressed the START button. Dick squeezed Ivy's sides gently and Ivy leaned forward into a trot.

Ivy trotted all the way around the ring. "What's the time?!" shouted Dick. Ann glanced at the watch.

"Forty-five seconds!" she called back. Dick clicked his tongue as a signal to Ivy. Ivy shook his creamy mane and gave out a whinny, then picked up speed. He cantered around the ring. Dick held on tight.

Halfway around the ring, Ivy splashed into a muddy puddle. For a moment, Ann stood gaping in disbelief. Then suddenly she realized what had happened. Ivy slipped, lost his footing and fell. Murky water splashed up and hit Ivy's shiny coat and mane. Ann screamed. Dick fell off and hit the soft ground.

Ann rushed over to Dick. "Are you alright?"

Dick slowly got up. "Yeah, I'm okay. Just a couple bruises. I've been thrown plenty of times, but never by Ivy."

"It wasn't his fault." Ann found herself defending Ivy.

"Yeah, I don't think it will happen again. I just got to watch out for that puddle."

"Is Ivy okay?"

"Wait, where is Ivy?" Dick looked around frantically. There was not a sign of his favorite horse. Frantically Ann scanned the field where they had been working. It would be simply horrid if they could not find Dick's favorite horse! But then, Ann thought she saw a figure in the woods out of the corner of her eye...

"There he is!" she cried.

Chapter Six: On the Left

Wondering why Ivy ran off so quickly worried the cousins. "We have to go find him!" Ann expressed her worry, hoping the muddy horse wasn't hurt.

"You're right! He won't go far. I wonder why he ran. I wonder what's wrong!"

Dick was confused by the troublesome situation. After taking his helmet off, Dick and Ann raced into the forest. Ivy's shoe prints were visible, thanks to all the mud from the early rain. Both cousins stopped, trying to listen for a sound, any sound that would lead them to Ivy. A whinny here and there, and a print for every step they took, he had to be close by!

"Over here!" Dick said, hoping that Ivy would not ignore his gentle calls.

"I see him!" Ann shouted.

"Come here, boy...come here," came the soft-toned voice of Dick, coaxing Ivy. Finally, Ivy was there. He was only about fifteen yards away from where they had first started looking.

"I don't think we should train anymore today..." Dick suggested.

"You're right. I think this scare was all he needed to quit training for a little while. I'm sure he'll start again with no regrets tomorrow!" Ann finished her sentence with confidence.

Dick and Ann put Ivy back in his stall. Dick gave him some extra straw and hay to eat. "Can we groom him?" Ann questioned, feeling dignified because of her new horse-task ability.

"Good idea, he's a mess," Dick agreed, adding, "Hopefully, he'll trust me after what happened today."

"It wasn't your fault, though," Ann interjected.

"I should have been more careful, and watched where I was going better. Though Ivy did slip, I feel partially responsible."

The two finished grooming him. Ivy had no trouble trusting them. Both went inside, and as they did so, Pam caught them in the entry-way.

"Want to help us make some blueberry pastries?" she asked politely.

"Sure, be right there! What are we going to be making exactly?" Ann knew blueberry would be the flavor!

"Muffins first, then pies and cakes...."

Ann was hoping she wouldn't get sick of blueberries after this experience. And Dick told his family about what had happened outside.

"It's only one and a half weeks till the competition. I don't know if I'll be ready!" Dick looked really disappointed.

"You mean if *we'll* be ready!" Ann cracked a smile.

"Are you going to enter?" Uncle Nick asked as he came into the kitchen.

Ann hesitated, she thought she wanted to, but did she really?

"I am thinking about it..." she looked down, knowing Dick would make sure she would.

"Did Ivy get hurt?" Pam asked as she busily washed the plump berries.

"I didn't particularly check. I should again. I will after lunch," Dick admitted.

"He didn't really seem like it." Ann tried to remember the whole situation, and how Ivy partially limped. Ann slyly brought it up, half worried. "He did sort of limp, didn't he Dick?"

"Uh, I'll check soon."

Ann helped wash the blueberries. It took nearly fifteen minutes, since there were so many blueberries in so many pails.

41

In the meantime, Ann put the muffins into the heated oven and Pam started lunch. Uncle Nick was grilling hotdogs, and Aunt Jane was putting together a healthy fruit salad (with blueberries!).

Pam made some cheesy potatoes which was one of Ann's favorite side dishes. Dick came in and startled Ann as she was washing her hands for lunch.

"Ann?" he asked.

"What?" Ann jumped.

"Oh, sorry, I just wanted to let you know lunch is ready. And afterwards let's go to the barn and check on Ivy," he said, leaving slowly.

Everyone was seated at the kitchen table, and the food looked great.

"Are you all packed for camp?" Aunt Jane asked Dick.

"Camp?" Ann felt obligated to say something, she knew nothing about this 'camp thing!'

"Yes, didn't you tell her, Dick?" Aunt Jane turned to look at her son.

"No, actually I didn't," was all the boy said. Ann could tell he felt bad.

Uncle Nick explained, "It's a boy's nature camp, for short they call it B.N.C. It's on Thursday through Monday morning."

"This Thursday?"Ann reached for the potatoes, "That's in only two days!"

"Pam will be here," Aunt Jane pointed out thoughtfully.

"But I won't be able to help you train while you're gone, then." Ann said.

"That's okay, because you can train without me." Dick set down his fork, "And when I get back, you'll already have started."

"Who will help me? Pam?" Ann asked worried.

"Sure thing!" Pam replied, glad to help her cousin.

"Thanks," Ann smiled.

The table was quiet until they finished eating.

"Ready to go, Ann?" Dick asked, putting his shoes on and grabbing his hat to shade him from the sun.

"All ready!" She did the same. They both went into the barn, and closed the heavy door. Some fresh air came in from the windows.

"Hey boy," Dick said, hoping nothing was wrong.

Ann opened the stall door. Ivy looked much better after his grooming. First, Dick checked Ivy's legs and inspected where he had fallen.

"Nothing I can see, although it's pretty dim in here. These clouds don't help." Dick then put his hands around the bottom part of Ivy's front leg. A whiny echoed through the barn. Ann stepped back, and for once, Dick did too.

In the meantime, Aunt Jane was looking for the chickens they had kept. Where were the four chickens they had not traded?!

"Ah-ha!" she said to herself. She found herself in the field near the fence, beyond that was some shady trees. There they were. She had found the missing four.

Aunt Jane gathered up the runaways and put them where they belonged. Wait, what was this? Another hole in the fence? "Now why is there a hole here? We don't have to worry about that neighbor dog getting to those chickens; Nick talked to the neighbor, and they are definitely not going to let the dog in again... Must be a fox who made this." Aunt Jane spoke out loud to herself.

Then, she tried to fix the hole and succeeded. The neighbor was putting an electric fence up so the dog would not escape and trespass again. Aunt Jane went back in and while the muffins were cooling started on a cake.

43

The cousins in the barn looked closer at the leg Ivy had fallen on. There was definitely something wrong with the left front leg. Dick tried to explain what he could tell from it.

"Is it sprained?" Ann asked.

Dick looked up at her, "More like... is it broken?"

Chapter Seven: The Right Horse

"Broken!" Ann exclaimed. "Are you certain?"

"No, I'm not positive. But when I felt there, he jumped so suddenly. He seems very sensitive there. I think Uncle Nick should look at this." Dick definitely sounded worried. The cousins ran into the house. "Dad! Dad!" Dick yelled. "Where are you?"

"I'm right here," Uncle Nick appeared. "What's the trouble?"

"It's Ivy. Out when I was riding, you know how I said he slipped?"

"Yeah?"

"Well, I think he broke his left front leg!"

Uncle Nick lost no time in going out to the barn. He inspected Ivy and when he felt Ivy's left front leg, Ivy reared up in pain.

"Whoa, boy!" Uncle Nick commanded. Ivy quieted down. Uncle Nick shook his head sadly. "It's broken alright," he said.

"Does that mean..." Dick began worriedly, but Uncle Nick cut him short.

"Afraid so, son. This horse ain't entering no competition."

"But it's in a week and a half. Maybe Ivy will recover."

"Doubt it," said Uncle Nick, "besides, even if he does, it wouldn't give you enough time to train him."

"Yeah," agreed Dick gloomily.

"Cheer up, son. You've got plenty of other horses you can enter."

"None of them are half as good as Ivy."

"Well, I'm gonna call a vet to look at this leg," Uncle Nick said, "Ivy needs a cast if it is broken and then again maybe the vet will say it isn't broken. But don't keep your hopes up too high," Uncle Nick told Dick. He then departed from the barn.

Ann stroked Ivy's soft coat. She didn't know what to say to Dick, he seemed pretty down. "He seems like a strong horse," Ann began nervously. "Maybe he'll recover."

"Maybe!?" Dick shouted out angrily as he stomped out of the barn.

What did I say? Ann wondered, a tear trickling down her cheek.

"It's alright, boy," Ann's voice quivered as she spoke to Ivy. She closed his stall door and went out of the barn. She looked around for Dick but saw him nowhere. So she went into the kitchen. The sweet aroma of cake filled the room.

"Have you seen Dick?" Ann asked her aunt.

"Yes, he went to his room. I wouldn't talk to him though, he seems pretty mad. Why'd you want to see him?"

"He… just got mad at me all of a sudden. I don't know what I said that made him so upset. I wanted to apologize. I just said Ivy was a strong horse and I thought he had a good chance of recovering," Ann tried to explain.

"He's just angry 'cause he cares a lot about that horse. It's the pride and joy of his life. He wants more than anything for that horse to win those competitions."

"I understand," Ann said solemnly.

Aunt Jane then said to Ann, "This cake should be done cooking in about ten minutes. While it cools, how about doing some quilting with Pam and me?"

"Sure!" Ann agreed. While waiting for the cake to finish Pam and Ann set up the sewing machine and set to picking out some cloth.

"This pattern is pretty," Ann fingered a rose-designed cloth.

"Or how about this?" Pam suggested an aqua colored one.

Ann picked out four more fabrics. Pam showed Ann how to cut nice even squares out of the cloths. Soon Aunt Jane joined them.

"Here, I'll show you how to start," Aunt Jane offered. Taking two squares she lined them up and pushed the sewing machine pedal. *Brrr...* went the sewing machine. She sewed a nice even line connecting the two. Ann then tried it herself. It came out rather crooked, but more attempts were made, and Ann got better with each one.

After an hour or so they had completed three rows across of the quilt. "We've made some good progress," Aunt Jane commented positively as she began picking up.

Ann asked, "Is Dick still in his room?"

"I think so," Pam replied.

Ann knocked on Dick's door.

"Who is it?" came Dick's muffled voice.

"Ann."

"Oh." Dick opened the door. He looked kind of embarrassed. "I...uh..." he did not quite know how to begin. "I didn't mean to shout at you." He made his apology.

"I forgive you," Ann said. "How about playing a game of Quiddler with me?"

"Sure, if you teach me how," Dick smiled his handsomest grin.

They sat down at the table. Ann brought out a game that she had brought with her. "It's kind of like Scrabble except on cards," Ann explained. After a while Dick got the hang of it. At the end of the game Dick had 214 points and Ann had 209.

"You won!" Ann cheered him.

"Just beginner's luck," Dick stated modestly. "It's a fun game though." As he spoke, Ann packed up the game.

"I'll... I'll miss you when you leave on Thursday." Ann tried to tell Dick how she thought he was a fun and exciting cousin.

"It won't be that long."

"Still..." Ann paused. "Ah... if you can't enter Ivy do you want me to help you train a different horse?"

"I don't know, maybe I'd better not enter at all."

Ann was surprised. "What about Lilac?" she suggested.

"She's Pam's horse. I've been thinking about it, maybe there will be a different competition when Ivy's better."

"Who knows? You might be passing up your only chance," Ann reminded him.

"Well, yes," Dick said. "I suppose I could enter Daylight, he's strong and fast. And good-looking."

After the burritos were finished Aunt Jane brought out the delicious blueberry cake she had prepared. It even had homemade cream cheese frosting on top. And on the side they had cookie dough ice cream. "I feel like it's somebody's birthday or something," Ann laughed. "All this dessert!"

"What if it is?" Dick asked, a mischievous twinkle in his brown eyes. Ann set her fork down.

"Wait...it isn't, right?"

"No, of course it isn't anybody's birthday," Dick laughed. "Though I sure had you fooled!"

Dessert being finished, they all helped clean up. When the work was done, Ann went to see what Ginger was doing. Ginger was curled up on her mat asleep. She looked so cute and innocent lying there. Just looking at her made Ann feel rather drowsy herself. She whispered, "Goodnight, Ginger." Then she softly placed a kiss on Ginger's head. After that Ann retired to bed.

The following morning was Wednesday. Ann woke at 6 o'clock to loud talking downstairs. Ann wondered what was wrong. Quickly dressing, she rushed down stairs. The family seemed to be in some state of confusion. They were looking about under things, in drawers, in every nook and corner. Evidently, something seemed lost.

"What's going on?" Ann asked curiously.

"Dad's lost his glasses, and nobody can find them," Dick explained.

"Well, where'd he see them last?" Ann tried to be of some help.

"When he went to bed he put them on the table in his room, or so he thought. But he was so tired he doesn't quite remember," Dick resumed his previous search accompanied by Ann.

Ginger began to bark. She wagged her tail back and forth excitedly. Then she ran to her mat and triumphantly carried back Uncle Nick's glasses in her teeth. Ann quickly snatched them back. She apologized for her mischievous dog, "I am *so* sorry about that."

Uncle Nick just nodded solemnly and went to clean his glasses.

"I hope nothing's broken."

They all went to the table and said a prayer. Ann began eating a warm, juicy blueberry muffin. Uncle Nick came over, with his glasses on. "At least they didn't break," he muttered.

"I am *terribly* sorry," Ann expressed her sympathy again, feeling rather guilty. "It won't happen again."

When breakfast was over Dick said, "I'm going to go check on the horses."

"Oh yeah," Uncle Nick recalled. "I forgot to tell you that the vet came yesterday."

"What did he say?" Dick asked.

"Well, that it *is* broken. He fixed a good cast up on Ivy. Sorry to be the bearer of bad news, son."

"It's okay," Dick tried to be cheerful, "I kind of expected it to be broken anyway."

Dick went to the barn and Ann followed. "Well," said Dick, "I've been thinking a lot. You're right. If I don't enter the competition I might be passing up my only chance. There aren't many chances like this. So I've finally decide to enter."

"Good!" Ann exclaimed, "I knew you would!"

"Do you want to enter too?"

"Yes, now I know that I do."

"Then let's find our horses and start training before I leave for camp!" Dick seemed excited.

In the barn, the cousins groomed and fed the horses. Ann was pretty sure she wanted to enter Autumn, but Dick was not so decided. He loved Ivy the best and it broke his heart to go with any other. "I don't know, Ann," Dick spoke slowly. "I thought before that Daylight would be right, but now I'm not so sure. What do you think Ann? Is Daylight really the right one?"

Chapter Eight: Tricky Training

Ann looked at the ground. She was unsure, but finally spoke up.

"Yes! I think you should... I mean why not? Of course there *is* Jewel and Crystal."

"That's a lot of help." Dick replied sarcastically.

"Jewel and Crystal... do they run fast or anything?"

"They are actually rather older horses. Not real old but I think they are fifteen. They are exactly the same age you know, because they are twins."

"Seems to me that Daylight would be a great choice then!"

"Daylight....he was a little wild. We got him from a neighbor that used to live around here and then moved. Certainly not so handsome as Ivy..." Dick certainly was in the mood for comparing every horse to how much better he thought Ivy was!

"Well that's for the judges to decide. Is he as fast as Ivy? Have you ridden him much?" Ann was full of questions.

"I've ridden him, not a lot, but he's fast. I'm not sure how fast, but I guess I'll find out when I saddle him up!"

The cousins unlatched the stall door and led the big horse out. It was then that Ann noticed how much larger Daylight was compared to Ivy, or any of the other horses for that matter. Ann was a bit frightened. "What...what did you mean when you said that Daylight was a bit wild? Does he bite or kick?"

"Oh no! I mean not anymore. He was not very tame when we got him , but he is tons better now. Nothing to worry about."

"Oh?" Ann was not sure about it still, her old fear of horses rushed through her.

Dick and Ann soon had Daylight saddled and ready. "Are you going to ride him in laps again?"

"No, I'll set up some barrels to weave through and after a while and he's warmed up we can try some jumping."

Dick was on Daylight in no time. Ann moved the heavy barrels around as Dick directed. Dick let Daylight walk for a while to get warmed up and practiced steering him around the barrels.

"So," ventured Ann. "Are you going to enter in all three competitions or just one of them?"

"Well, I know we don't have much time. Daylight is in good condition though."

"So?"

"Perhaps, we'll work on jumping and racing, I mean not that Daylight isn't pretty, he well... I don't know, maybe just jumping?" Dick seemed confused and didn't know what to say.

Ann tried to comfort him. "I know that you love Ivy. He's a real good horse, but you have to put your mind on Daylight and train him."

"Right."

Dick gave a slight kick with his heels and Daylight trotted around the arena. Ann could tell Dick was definitely wasn't happy. After a while Dick told Ann that he was going to ride Daylight down the trails for a bit. Ann walked back to the house, turning the matter over in her mind.

How am I going to enter a horse in a week and a half when it's been like five years since I've ridden, and I don't even have Dick to help me? Perhaps all this horse stuff is too much and I should just watch.. Yet I told Dick I wanted to enter, but well, do I?

Uncle Nick and Pam weren't in the house, but Aunt Jane was there. "How's your training coming along?" she asked.

How is it coming along? Ann thought to herself.

"I've not even rode a horse the whole time I've been here! I guess Dick's doing fine. He went out on a trail ride with Daylight. Since, well *you* know, 'cause of Ivy's accident."

"Do you want me to help you ?" Aunt Jane asked.

"Help me what?" Ann was surprised.

"Train of course. You know, it's not just Dick who likes horses. I don't go very fast, but I can ride Crystal. I can teach you about steering and things."

"Oh would you?" Ann was delighted. She hadn't even imagined Aunt Jane *could* ride! How silly of her!

Aunt Jane proved to be a good teacher, and although Ann was nervous and unsure, she was at last in the saddle on Crystal's back. She wanted to enter Autumn, but since Aunt Jane knew Crystal the best, they both thought it good to get started with her.

Crystal took a step forward. Aunt Jane was holding the halter as she led Crystal around with Ann mounted in the saddle. Ann gripped the horn on the saddle. Was she *really* doing this? Ann's helmet slid to one side so Ann adjusted it to be tighter.

"Sit up straight and look forward." Aunt Jane instructed. Ann followed her advice. "Now, I'm going to adjust your stirrups. They are a bit short."

Ann moved her foot out of the way while Aunt Jane adjusted.

Aunt Jane led Crystal slowly around. Ann's heart was pounding. She tried to calm herself. *Everything is going to be fine,* she kept repeating to herself.

"Put your weight in your heels and point your heels down toward the ground," Aunt Jane advised. Crystal snorted and shook her neck. "Now, now, girl." Aunt Jane spoke softly to the horse and then to Ann, "They like gentle voices." All too soon Aunt Jane said she was going to let Ann try by herself, which meant Aunt Jane would not be holding the lead rope. Aunt Jane stepped off to the side under some shady trees.

Ann had never been more scared in her life. Well, maybe the time when she was going down the roller coaster was more scary. Or the time the horse she was riding when she was little ran away from the guide. She had been very scared, then.

A slight kick made Crystal begin to walk. Ann held her reins tight and close to her. "Loosen your reins, let your hands rest on Crystal's neck," Aunt Jane said. If it weren't for Aunt Jane being there, Ann had no idea what she would do. Thank goodness for Aunt Jane!

"Now steer towards the barrels by letting the rein rest on the side of her neck and moving your hand that way. Yes, that's it. Good for you!" Aunt Jane praised. Ann still was frightened but was feeling more accustomed to the riding after a while. Dick came back on Daylight in about fifteen minutes.

"You're in the saddle! Congratulations!" laughed Dick who seemed in better spirits after his morning ride.

"Thanks," smiled Ann very nervously. Crystal stopped and shifted her weight letting out a sigh.

"Do you want to ride some trails?" Dick asked.

"I just got up here, I...I don't know," Ann stammered, looking to Aunt Jane for help.

"I think it is a fine idea," remarked Aunt Jane, "A lot of people go on trails even if they have never ridden a horse before." That's not exactly what Ann had wanted to hear.

"Isn't Daylight tired though?" Ann asked, "Doesn't he need to rest?"

"Nah, he wouldn't be much of a horse if he couldn't do another ride. Come on, let's go. We'll take it real slow and I'll go in front and Crystal can just follow along. Maybe tomorrow you'll want to saddle up Autumn."

Daylight trotted up to Crystal and put his nose to hers. Dick steered Daylight away. "These horses are buddies, but it's not a good idea for any horses to get too close to each other." Dick chose another trail and began to walk his horse down it. Crystal followed; plodding slowly behind.

Dick said nothing for a while, and Ann found there was nothing for her to say, so the two riders continued on in silence. The day was getting hot and the summer sun beat down upon them. Ann's throat yearned for water. She was thinking about asking to turn around. The dusty trail did not help.

Presently they came to a large hill. Ann felt it a good place to ask about heading back, when she saw it! At first, Ann wasn't sure what *it* was. There was something on top of the hill, her first thought was that it was a deer. Yet it was too big for that and yet too far away to tell...was it a horse? Or were Ann's eyes deceiving her?

Dick seemed to notice it as well. He urged Daylight to canter up the hill. Ann didn't even think about her dry throat and forgot her nervousness as she urged Crystal up the hill after Dick. She held on tight and leaned forward as Dick told her to.

Yet, as the two adventurers ascended the animal noticed them and vanished down the other side of the hill. Where had it gone? And, more like, what was it?!

Chapter Nine: Lost and Found

Dick and Ann both slowed down, Ann was still in earnest though of what the creature could have been. "What was it?" she started to say, thinking maybe Dick had seen it before or recognized it from a previous time. Both cousins came to a halt.

"Well, it definitely was big. Bigger than any deer..." he paused a moment to think. "It could be a horse that got loose from one of the neighbors, or... or wild!" Ann stopped. Her mind froze, she had never seen an actual wild horse!

"Are they very dangerous?" Ann was prone to worry.

"I've never been face to face with one or have been this close to one, like we might have been just now! They could definitely be very dangerous, but it depends on its surroundings. Plus if it was hurt, or hungry and thirsty..." Ann was absorbing the information cautiously.

"My grandfather, he use to tame wild horses." Dick said, sounding rather proud.

"Really?" Ann sounded amazed and intrigued. "Is he still alive?" she then asked.

"No, actually...he died a few years back. I think he got a rare sickness. But he would catch wild horses in these same woods, tame them, and sell to buyers." Ann could tell Dick wanted to have a job like his grandfather's.

"Were you two close?" his cousin asked, always sensitive to another's feelings.

"Kind of, he lived just down the road a few miles. I never got to go with him on any of his taming adventures. Heard plenty of stories, though."

"Oh….I bet they were good stories, too!" Ann comforted. "Did he ever get hurt from a wild horse?" Once again, she was trying not to worry.

"My grandpa? Never. He was an expert!" Dick replied as he looked far off into the hills.

The two started on the trail once more. Ann was getting used to the idea and feel of riding. She said, "Did he keep any of the wild horses that he tamed?" Her cousin slowed down, now they were side by side.

"I don't know... he did give my father some horses, awhile back, when he died. I was only six, I forgot how long ago it was!"

"Wow! So you wouldn't really remember much." Ann was riding very gracefully, she felt like a professional. They had probably been gone for about half an hour more, it really didn't feel that long though.

"I've never been on this trail," Dick stated.

"Do you know where we're going?" Ann needed to be reassured.

"Of course. It's a trail, so it's marked and all cleared. This is where my grandpa used to live..." said Dick. "My grandma decided to move when he died... she lives about 45 miles or so away from here. Actually, I think she is going to visit in a week or something.

"Really? Cool!" Ann exclaimed looking at the charming yellow farmhouse a little bit of a distance off.

"She lives with her son," Dick pointed out.

Once more, the cousins stopped. This time Ann started the conversation.

"What is this farmhouse, now? Is it still part of your grandpa's property?" she asked.

"I believe so!" Dick continued, "I've actually never seen it before, it is definitely within his acreage, though. I wonder..."

"What? Does anyone else live there now?" Ann said.

"No one lives there. We own it, because my grandma sold it cheaply to us when she moved. I'm in the mood for exploring. How 'bout you?" Dick asked. He dismounted his horse and tied it to a thick birch tree.

"Kind of."Ann followed her cousin's lead, wondering what kind of adventure it would be this time. Ann was part unsure, more like mostly unsure, part excited.

There was also a small wooden cabin-like structure. Although it looked old, it seemed sturdy and secure. "Let's check out this cabin/shed thing. It was for sure grandpa's, just I don't know what he used it for. We may eventually sell it, not sure, though. I think my grandma wants Pam to inherit it when she is older, but who knows how that situation will go," Dick sounded unsure. When they both reached the shed, Dick turned the doorknob. Ann followed along, trusting.

Upon opening the door, Ann stepped back, hoping for it to be cleared and uncluttered. It was a very cute space, Ann soon found. There were quaint built-in shelves and drawers. A few pictures lined the walls. Ann began to get in an exciting mood as she opened a drawer.

An old picture in a hand-made wooden frame lay alone in the spacious drawer. "Dick, look at this, is it your grandpa?" Ann asked picking up the picture. He came over to where she stood in the bright light from the window.

"Was this one of his horses? A wild one maybe?" Ann was excited.

"Maybe it says somewhere, look on the back!" Dick suggested. He was intrigued himself. His cousin took his advice. There was something inscribed on the back.

"It says..." Ann paused. "It says: 'Grandpa saves a baby horse from abandonment. He names it Autumn.' Why Dick, Autumn!"

"What?!" Dick exclaimed, hardly believing his own ears. "He saved Autumn's life, my grandfather did!"

Ann was very surprised herself, *amazed* at their discovery. "I wonder if he tamed some of the other horses..." Dick pondered aloud.

"Hmm...maybe your grandma knows. Hey, maybe when she comes to visit, and you get back from camp, you can ask her. I bet she'll remember!"

"Yes, she probably would!" Dick agreed happily.

"This would be the perfect place for a hideout or something!" Ann introduced her interesting idea. "When you get back from your BNC, we can ride here, and come play in here!" His excited cousin set the picture back in the drawer. "I wonder if your grandmother wants this picture."Ann thought aloud, adding this new idea to her 'ask grandma' list.

"Yeah, maybe. When I get back from camp I'll come out here with you if you want, and maybe we could do some training!" Dick added to Ann's previous idea.

Ann felt better about the whole horse situation. "Do you want to do what your grandfather did, with the horses and all?" A trace of wonder reacted in his face.

"Yeah, I mean, he was an expert. I don't... I just don't know if I'd be brave enough." Ann could tell he had thought about it plenty.

"We should probably head back now!" said punctual Ann. Dick agreed, very glad they had found part of his grandpa's past. Ann had never really known her grandparents either. She felt a little jealous.

They went back outside, closed the door, and then they saw it!

"Dick! Dick!" Ann whispered harshly as she tapped his shoulder, since he was turned because he had closed the door. "The animal!"

He suddenly turned around.

"A horse! It's a horse! It looks wild too!" Dick whispered excitedly to Ann, trying not to startle the beautiful wild-looking creature.

Ann got very excited, she knew what Dick was thinking of at this moment. He would want to catch and tame that horse! It was a beautiful tall and black horse, just gorgeous. It's mane blew in the soft breeze. Ann wanted to bring her camera next time. Pam and the rest of the family had to see this!

"Dick, what are you thinking?" Ann pried.

"I wonder," he started as the black mystery horse galloped down a hill, "I wonder if that, with the help of Uncle Nick, we could catch it."

"We?" Ann asked. "Well I don't know..."

They both got on their horses. Ann still couldn't believe that Autumn, the horse she would probably enter in the competition, used to be wild.

Dick seemed to be very proud of Ann's horse skills, so was Ann. She couldn't believe how she found the courage to actually do it! Aunt Jane had helped a lot too that morning. They arrived home, very tired from their experience. Lunch was already on the table when they came in. They had already put their horses back in their stalls. Aunt Jane asked about the cousins' ride as they came into the house, very thirsty.

"It was great!" Ann began to say, but Dick cut her off quickly. He was super excited because of the wild horse. As everyone sat down, Ann thanked Aunt Jane for helping her that day. It had come in handy.

Dick explained to Uncle Nick that they saw a wild horse, and explored his grandfather's hut. A surprised uncle paused, but just for a moment. "You saw what?!" He got a little worked up, because it is always good to be safe.

"Yeah, Dad! And Autumn use to be a wild horse, well, kind of still is. Grandpa tamed her!" Dick exclaimed. Uncle

Nick did not want to break his son's excitement. "Could you help me catch it, and, and tame it?" Dick asked breathlessly. Silence awoke. "Like grandpa?" Dick thought aloud.

They rest of lunch was ate in silence. Dick then went to his room to start packing. His dad didn't answer his question. He thought about it non-stop. Would the black mystery ever be solved?

Chapter Ten: Dark Trouble

Dick folded a shirt and shoved it in his backpack. He was frustrated. Why hadn't his father answered him? He wanted to follow his grandfather's example and tame the black horse, but he couldn't do it alone. He wondered if while he was away the black horse would run far away and Dick would never see him again. Then his dream of taming him would be impossible...

Meanwhile Ann went with Pam to get the mail. "Oh! Look, Ann. There's a letter for you!" Pam exclaimed.

"For me?" Ann seemed a bit shocked. Pam handed her an envelope. "Oh, it's from my parents," Ann spoke as she opened the envelope. She read the following:

Dear Ann,

We were delighted to hear you are enjoying yourself. Everything is well here. Danny's team won the softball game last night! He's very proud. Their team has a golden trophy. As to the question of a pet rabbit, I and your father have come to the conclusion that you may have one if you like. You'll have to find or buy a cage and food there. I hope you have fun.

Love,
Mom and Dad

The letter was short, but warmly received. Ann was excited at the prospect of getting a rabbit. Hopefully, Pam's friends still had some. She was also proud of her little brother.

Ann walked into the house with Pam, telling Pam about the letter. Dick met them in the house. "What's up?" he inquired. Ann told him of her letter. "Good for you," he said, but somehow his tone hinted at a bit of angriness.

"Uncle Nick still hasn't answered you yet, has he?" Ann asked cautiously.

"No, he hasn't." Dick sighed impatiently. "But I don't know if we actually could catch the horse. I mean my grandpa was an expert. I'm just a kid and inexperienced, know what I mean?'"

"Yeah, but I could help you," Ann paused. "I know very little about horses but together perhaps we could catch and tame the black horse."

"Not without Dad's help," Dick reminded her.

"Yeah, I guess," Ann admitted.

"Are you all packed?" Ann changed the subject.

"Yeah," said Dick. He paused a minute, a mischievous grin spreading across his tanned face. "Ann," he began slowly, "maybe you're right. Maybe you can help me catch that horse."

"What do you mean?" Ann was confused.

"Come out to the barn," Dick looked secretive.

The two cousins went to the barn. Ann was puzzled. Dick grabbed Daylight's halter. "What are you doing?" Ann was curious. They had just gone on a long trail ride. Dick said nothing and saddled up Daylight. He tied the large horse to a pole. Then he got Autumn and saddled her up. He handed the halter to Ann.

"Where *are* we going?" Ann asked.

"To catch that horse."

"What?" Ann asked as he led the horses out of the barn. "How do you intend to do that?"

"With these," Dick snatched a rope and presented a bucket of oats as they left the barn. Ann was still confused. "Let me explain." Dick said with an air of importance, "We may just be kids, but Dad ain't so much the horse type, so I don't know if he'd want to help us. I reckon it can't be that hard."

"Well, I suppose..." Ann had a guilty feeling about all this as she got in her saddle. It felt different than sitting on Crystal. "Shouldn't we tell someone where we are going?" Ann asked as they started off. Ann noticed how Autumn's walk had a different feel.

"Nope," was all Dick said.

Down the trail they rode, winding here and there. Dick urged Daylight forward into a trot. Ann gave Autumn a slight squeeze. She quickened into a fast trot. Ann had no control and Autumn was going off the trail. "Whoa girl!" Ann pulled the reigns. Her heartbeat quickened. Where was Dick? Ann steered Autumn back onto the path. "Dick? Where are you?" Ann's voice bounced off the trees, an eerie sound echoed all around her. Ann was scared to death. "Dick!?" she shouted. Autumn's ears twitched and she stomped her foot. "It's okay, girl, at least I think so." Ann patted Autumn's neck.

Dick suddenly appeared over the hill on his mount. "There you are," Ann sighed a sigh of relief. "Don't go running off like that. We could get separated even more than we did."

"Sorry." Dick apologized. "I forgot you just started riding."

"It's all right."

They stuck together as they continued on the trail. "Look! Up ahead!" Ann breathed. The beautiful black horse stood on the trail just up ahead. His glossy black coat bathed in the sun.

"Black Mystery," Dick whispered.

"Huh?" Ann was confused.

"That's what I've named him," came the reply.

"Oh, fits him perfectly," Ann agreed.

Dick on Daylight walked a little closer to Black Mystery. The horse turned his head to look at the approaching rider. Dick stopped short. Black Mystery reared and galloped off into the distance. Soon he was out of sight. "Wow, can he run," Dick spoke with disappointment. "It might not be so easy catching him as I thought."

The cousins continued riding. The warm summer breeze hushed through the trees. A chipmunk chattered noisily. The birds chirped in the trees. The steady clomp of the horses' hoofs sounded rhythmically. Yet there was no sign of Black Mystery.

"There's the hut." Ann pointed out where they had ventured on their last adventure and where they had found some of Dick's grandfather's things. They rode by it, deeper into the woods. Out this far even Dick had not ventured...

The trees began to grow denser and the long grass brushed against the horse's legs. The place had plenty of biting flies. Then, something lay before them: a silvery lake sparkling like crystals, and on the other side was Black Mystery! He evidently had swum across for he was dripping wet.

"Now what do we do?" Ann asked, a little annoyed.

"We could swim across on our horses."

"I don't think I'm ready for that yet."

"It's really not that hard, you just ride and then pull your feet out of the stirrups putting them on the horse's shoulders. The horse does the rest; just swims across." It still didn't sound all that easy to Ann.

"Black Mystery will probably just bolt off again though," Ann said.

"Yeah, but...I got another idea." Slowly Dick climbed off Daylight. He set the pail of oats on the ground. Remounting Daylight he rode off into the trees. Ann followed him.

"What are you expecting to happen?" Ann asked.

"That horse will be curious and come and eat the oats. Then all we gotta do is put the rope on him." But Black Mystery was busy chewing a clump of grass on the other side of the lake and paying no attention to the bucket.

Daylight eyed the oats hungrily, but Dick held him back. "Here boy," he said giving the horse a chunk of carrot, that had been in his saddlebags. Autumn was jealous, nudging Dick for her share. "Okay girl," Dick laughed holding out a different carrot chunk. Autumn gently lifted the carrot from his palm.

They watched Black Mystery. He didn't even seem to take any notice at all of them or the bucket of oats. Or anything else besides his grass! After all, what was it to him? He was a wild horse who lived on the wild things. He'd never seen or eaten a bucket of oats. Dick left his mount and emerged from the trees. Black Mystery turned to look at him. He snorted and continued eating. Dick sighed and picked up the oats. Coming back to Daylight, he let the horse eat from the bucket.

"That horse won't eat these oats. Guess it was kind of a stupid idea. He *is* wild."

"At least you tried," Ann said.

"Well, I gotta do better than just try. I've *got* to catch him," Dick was very determined.

"What time is it?"Ann inquired.

"Five," Dick glanced at his watch. Ann was surprised at how late it was getting. She was a little uneasy.

"Shouldn't we be getting back for dinner? I mean people might be getting worried," Ann feared.

"What's there to worry about? They'll see the horses gone and know we went on a trail ride."

"I'm getting kind of hungry." Even as Ann spoke the sun seemed to sink lower in the sky and it began to darken.

"Shh...look, Black Mystery's coming across to this side," Dick whispered, rope in hand. The black horse reached the shore on their side. He shook his wet body, sending water droplets in every direction. He moved closer to the children.

Dick made a loop in the rope and swung it out at the horse. It lashed out like lightning and hit the horse's rear leg. Rearing up in pain, the horse bolted off back the way it came. "I meant to get it over his head. Guess I don't have very good aim," Dick said.

Then, all of a sudden, thunder rumbled in the sky and it grew dark. "Looks like a storm, we'd better be getting back," Dick said. It began to rain. Lightning flashed in the sky. Daylight jumped up in fright. Dick talked soothingly to him, trying to quiet him down.

Dick and Ann started back on their horses. The rain fell heavily and it was so dark it was hard to see. "This is strange," Dick said, "Storms don't usually come up this fast. Stay close, so we don't get lost." Ann was frightened. Before long the sky became pitch dark and the riders could see nothing.

"Dick!" Ann yelled.

Chapter Eleven: A Frightful Night

Oh, Ann had to find her cousin before it was too late! If she couldn't find him, well, oh she didn't even want to think about it! "Dick! Oh Dick!" she frantically called into the darkness. "Please don't go anywhere Dick, I am so scared. Oh, what are we going to do?" Ann pat Autumn's wet neck.

Autumn was trotting, but Ann had no idea where they were going. It was so bumpy! Dick was there just a second ago. Oh, where was Daylight? What they needed was real daylight!

"Whoa, girl." Ann stopped Autumn; it was no good to go anywhere you couldn't see! Ann pressed her lips together. "Dick!" Ann called once more, nervously. The rain soaked Ann's skin and her clothes were heavy and wet. The saddles squeaked when Ann shifted her weight. Ann was so tired and not to mention starving. It had been a long day. It was still her first day of riding, and here she was-all alone!

Ann wanted to cry, but at that moment she heard her cousin's boyish voice calling, "Ann!" It seemed distant, yet it gave her hope. Ann let Autumn follow Dick's voice, or at least Ann *hoped* Autumn was following Dick's voice.

Quite suddenly and unexpectedly, there was a cold splash and water was around Ann's already cold legs and boots. Autumn had gone into the lake! Ann's jean pant legs clung to her legs and Ann's teeth chattered. She somehow managed to pull her legs out of the water and stirrups. "I just hope you're going the right way, baby," Ann shivered. Ann hoped Autumn was a good swimmer. She, herself was not.

"Keep going," Ann encouraged. It seemed to take hours for Autumn to swim that lake. At last they reached the other side. Ann was even more wet, if that was possible. And

Autumn was soaked, but for the tense situation, seemed to be taking it well. At least *she* wasn't panicking. Ann wondered if being a wild horse helped. She wondered about Black Mystery, what was he doing? How could a wild horse shelter from the rain? She wondered many things about the black wild horse, if indeed that's what he was. It certainly seemed to be, but she supposed it could be that someone lost their horse.

As Autumn plodded on, Ann thought.

Is Black Mystery a girl? Or a boy? How old is he? Ann figured Black Mystery was a perfect name; they hardly knew anything about him, except the obvious of course. He was black and beautiful.

Ann felt hopelessly lost. She thought about long night hours waiting for morning light. She thought about no dinner, and no breakfast. She thought about how long it would take for someone to find her. Ann thought about a lot of things. None of them seemed pleasant. She tried to keep her spirits up and held on to the hope that Autumn would somehow know the way. Ann couldn't understand how the horse could tell how not to bump into a tree or stumble on sharp rocks.

A sudden flash of lightening struck brightly across the sky, and for a moment the ground and trees were visible in the bright light. Yet only for a moment, and then the resounding clap of thunder echoed on.

Autumn put her ears back and quickened her pace frightened by the storm. Ann wondered what it was like to be a baby wild horse and be abandoned. Why would Autumn's mother leave her? Was she killed? Ann thought about how old Autumn was. If Dick was six when his grandfather died and gave some horses to Uncle Nick, and Dick was 14 now...that made Autumn at least 8. If an old horse was around 15, Autumn was still pretty middle aged and...

Ann's thoughts were interrupted by a loud neigh. It was pretty close. It wasn't Autumn though, maybe it was Daylight!

Ann called once more, "Dick? Daylight? Where are you?" No answer but the wind and rain. Ann was getting tired of the horrid blackness. It was empty and cold and lonely. The knot in Ann's stomach grew bigger. She was starving. "Dick!" cried Ann at the top of her lungs. Her dry throat seemed to be whipped away with the harsh biting wind.

A voice from behind surprised Ann, "Are you alright, cousin?"

Back at home, Aunt Jane was ready to call the police and was desperately fighting back hot tears. Uncle Nick stomped back and forth across the floor, his face knit in a frown. Pam was worried and stressed, yet managed to keep her cool. Aunt Jane sat in her living room chair next to a low-down side table with the home phone. She wrung her hands, "Nicholas, let me call the police!" she pleaded. "I'm so worried. They've been gone for hours, and that horrible storm..." she broke off sobbing about Dick and Ann.

"I'll go look for them," stated Uncle Nick gruffly.

"No! Papa, don't!" cried Pam, "I mean *you'll* get lost. Wouldn't it be better if you stayed?"

"No." Her father, with a sternly set face, got on his long green button-up coat. He went out the front door into the night with a flashlight, first aid supplies, cell phone, and knife.

"You're father is so stubborn," Aunt Jane threw up her hands helplessly.

"Perhaps, he will go to the old farmhouse. You know the one grandpa used to own? Maybe Dick and Ann are there." Pam held on to her new hope.

"Oh, is it really you Dick?! Truly?" Ann loudly shouted, feeling overjoyed.

"Course, dear cousin," Dick sounded calm, which was totally surprising to Ann. "Now then," Dick thrust a coarse piece of rope into Ann's shaking hands. "Hold on to it. Better yet, tie it to Autumn and she'll follow Daylight."

"Where are we going?" Ann curiously questioned.

Dick didn't answer for a while. He was thinking. *It is all my fault! I was being so proud; wanting to catch that horse all by myself. I didn't really think Ann would help much, but now... what a mess we are in!*

"Where are we going?" Ann repeated her question.

"Huh? Oh, that, uh..." Dick tried to think of a suitable response. He didn't really know.

"What about that farmhouse?" Ann suddenly remembered.

"Sure, if we can find it."

Gradually the rain let up. It was still bitterly wet and cold. Plus, there was black darkness. There was no moon or stars. The wet, heavy, thick clouds covered them all. "Somehow, we've got to find that lake, and cross it!" Ann spoke energetically. She was enthusiastic about the idea of going to the farmhouse to shelter.

At last some clouds cleared and the two could see easier. Luckily, they weren't far from the lake. Soon the children could see the dark trees and thick clouds in the shining reflection of the crystal clear water. Once more, they crossed the lake. And as they crossed it, Dick said, "You know Ann, you're doing really good! I mean you're great at riding horses!"

"You really think so?"

"Yeah. When I started, well ah… how 'bout we don't talk about that," Dick changed his mind.

"Why not?"

"It's kind of embarrassing."

Yet Ann couldn't help wondering about it. She wanted to ask what happened, but she didn't think Dick would want her to pry, so she let him be.

Finally, they had crossed the lake without too much trouble and were heading up the bank. Ann felt numb. She would give anything to be at Blueberry Ridge right now, eating one of Pam's warm filling dinners.

"Wait a sec," Dick paused and Daylight came to a stop.

"What is it?"

"Nothing, I..." Ann heard a whinny and sounds coming from nearby bushes. What was it?

"It's Black Mystery," whispered Dick.

"I know," breathed Ann. But where? They knew not. Although this was not the time to catch him, Ann wished she could see him. She still marveled at her love for horses. What had come over her? She had once feared them so much, even just a few days ago.

The mysterious horse seemed to be near them, yet soon they heard no more from the black horse. Ann felt extremely drowsy. She had to shake herself from falling asleep. The two adventurous cousins traveled a very long time. Suddenly, they saw a bright light far off in the distance.

"What can it be?" Dick asked aloud, nudging Ann, who was falling asleep again.

"Huh, what? What is it?" Ann asked, her eyes half open.

"I don't know! See the light?!" Dick pointed.

"Oh," Ann raised her sleepy eyes to gaze at the strange light.

"Dick! Ann!" a distant familiar voice called.

"Oh, hurry Ann!" Dick encouraged. "It's Dad."

72

"Really?" Ann tried to hurry her horse, yet her legs were so sore...

Chapter Twelve: Front Page

Ann managed to catch up to her cousin, who was now safely next to his father. "I'm so glad you two are safe. We were worried sick! Especially my wife!" Ann was so glad to be with her uncle, who knew the trails very well, even in the dark of the storm.

Then they all heard something. "Black Mystery?" Dick said looking up abruptly.

"Black who?" Uncle Nick had no idea what his son was talking about.

"The wild horse..." Dick's voice barely made it to his father's ears.

"'Are you telling me... no, you would never! You came out here to catch that wild beast! Oh, and you brought your innocent cousin along, too!" Uncle Nick sounded very angry.

Black Mystery seemed to be coming closer. Uncle Nick cooled his temper, and the three headed for home. Suddenly they heard a painful cry, the black beauty was hurt! Ann, still wet, cold, and hungry looked around, trying to tell where the injured horse might be. "We have to help, Dad. I know a hurt horse when I hear one!" Dick pleaded, he sounded like a horse expert. Uncle Nick knew what to do... he did bring first aid supplies, in case one of the children got hurt.

Uncle Nick pointed a direction, almost straightforward. "Here, this way," he said. Slowly but surely, he walked carefully through the darkened mist. "Look!" Dick got down from Daylight.

"Oh, no! He's laying down, hurt!" Ann explained what she saw. Uncle Nick went to the horse. Ann followed, slowly and carefully, wanting to be of some help.

"My fault..." said a very quiet Dick, then louder. "I did it, it was my fault! When I tried to catch him, I hit his leg instead!"

"Blood," is all Dick's father managed to say, while Ann helped Dick unpack the first aid. Ann was very scared of what a wild horse would do. *Is Black Mystery wild, though?* She questioned herself.

Uncle Nick bandaged the leg up, not too loose, nor too tight. The horse could barely stand, let alone, walk. Uncle Nick led it, slowly and smoothly, guiding it through the storm, still wondering what to do. Then Ann spoke her mind.

"What if he's not wild." She paused then to say, "It could be lost or something!"

Dick's father had a sure-response for that statement, "I'll call the horse rescue in the morning." Everyone stayed silent; Dick hoped no one would take "his" horse away!

Finally, they made it back. Aunt Jane came running outside. She didn't even care that there were puddles, for the storm still lingered in the air. Uncle Nick took Black Mystery into the barn, unlocking an empty stall. Ann kept her distance, although she was very proud of what she did that day.

After eating a late supper at about eight or a little later, Dick said goodbye to Ann and the rest of his family. He was leaving for camp, bright and early the next morning, and probably wouldn't have a chance to say goodbye then. "Bye, Ann! Take good care of our horse, don't let him be taken away!" her cousin whispered. Ann gave him a reassuring look.

Before going to bed Ann asked, "Are there any bunnies left? I got permission to get one!" She squealed excitedly, now conversing with her older cousin.

"That's good! I think there are three left!" Pam congratulated her cousin.

Ann awoke the next day, missing Dick already! She got up, and saw a note on her desk. It read:

-Ann,

I could enter Black Mystery in the competition, train him for me.

-Bye!

Dick

Ann smiled and set it back down. "I'll try Dick, I'll try." Going down for breakfast without Dick felt odd. She felt some humor had escaped the house. Uncle Nick appeared in the doorway from dropping him off.

"Mornin' Sweet Pea!" Uncle Nick didn't seem angry anymore about the so-called "wild horse". "I called the horse rescue, they said they only specialize in more major injuries." Uncle Nick sounded a little confused. Ann rejoiced inside, Dick would be so happy.

A newspaper slopped on the ground, outside the door. Ann opened the paper to preview it. The front page made her gasp, the headline read: "Missing Circus horse!" The picture was Black Mystery!

"Uncle Nick!" Ann exclaimed loudly handing him the paper, worried and stunned.

"Here's the number. I'll call."

Ann almost felt bad she pointed it out. It would have been found out anyway, she tried to comfort herself.

Pam brought in a baby bunny, cradled in her arms. "The three left were all brown," she said, softly handing Ann the small creature. Ann had sent Pam to pick out which one to have, since Ann was an indecisive person. Pam set the bunny in a cage with food. Ann named her Clover. Uncle Nick came into the room. Ann nervously urged him to speak.

"Seems they don't want him..." His eyes were squinted in wonder. "He acted so wild and now that he's hurt..."

Ann felt herself calm down. "I'll tame him up!" Confidence bellowed from her mouth, in place for Dick and partially herself.

Ann, during breakfast, understood greatly why Dick would want to enter Black Mystery. *He's gorgeous, amazingly fast, and probably can jump, he's in great shape!* Ann would try her best! After breakfast, Ann went out into the barn, with permission. She wanted to see how the horse was.

"How are ya, boy?" Ann soothed. At first she was afraid to touch him, but soon overcame her fear as she softly smoothed his neck.

The cut was well-bandaged. She had to let Dick know he wasn't wild! She needed to make sure Dick would enter Black Mystery. She felt that it was her job, and she was gonna do it right! The other horses were jealous of the attention, so Ann went and did the same to them.

She went to play with Clover then. Ginger yapped, apparently not too fond of baby rabbits. Soon, Ann decided she should write a letter to her parents, for she was eager to tell about Black Mystery. She wrote:

Dear Mom and Dad,

Thank you! I got the bunny today! I named her Clover. She is small and brown, super cute! Dick went to camp today. We also saved a hurt wild horse that ended up to be from the circus!

Thank you for the letter, I look forward to seeing you all soon!

Love you,

Ann

P.S. Tell Danny, great job at his game!

She put a stamp on her letter, kissed it, and put it in the mail box. She missed her family, but she also had family here, right now! Ann entered the house again; it was very hot outside.

"How quick do you think Mystery's leg will heal?" Ann inquired. She called him Mystery for short. As she worried about the answer destined to come, Ann wondered, would she have enough time to train both horses? And she knew hardly anything about training!

The question clouded her mind, but only for a moment. "Oh, not long. Should be about cleaned up by tomorrow," was the sure response from her uncle. Ann breathed a sigh of relief...

Chapter Thirteen: Warming Up

Ann started to do some of the morning chores with Pam: cleaning horse stalls, milking the cows, feeding the pigs, etc. Once they had finished, Pam questioned Ann. "How would you like some more riding practice?"

"Sure thing! I certainly need it!" Ann said, laughing.

Ann and her cousin saddled up Autumn and Lilac.

"Is Lilac fast?" asked Ann.

"Oh, not so fast, so I don't think I'll be entering in the upcoming competition. But, you know, the most important part is to have fun!" Pam added with emphasis.

Before getting on their horses, they practiced some lunging to get the horses worked up. Then, they got on. Ann squeezed Autumn into a walk. Ann tried to sit erect in the saddle, putting her weight in her heels, as Aunt Jane had directed yesterday.

"You're doing great!" Pam encouraged. "Ready for some trotting?"

"Ah, sure." Ann spoke a little unsurely though. Pam set Lilac into a trot. Autumn began trotting after her. It was bouncy and hard to control Autumn.

"Try going up and down in your saddle as she trots. Sort of stand up in your stirrups every time she bounces up," Pam helpfully suggested. Ann found that when she did that, it helped.

Pam and Ann got off their horses. While they groomed them, Ann thought she smelled something funny. What was it? Smoke? Ann smelled smoke! Something was burning. Ann glanced at Pam. "I think it's coming from the barn!" she exclaimed. With much worry, they left their horses tied to the trees.

Rushing to the barn, Pam pulled open the doors. Smoke bellowed out and flames leaped everywhere. "Quick, Ann! Get Dad!" Pam coughed. Ann was already on her way...

She burst into the house. "Uncle Nick! Uncle Nick!" Ann yelled. She could not find him anywhere. Aunt Jane was nowhere to be found either! Frantically, she rushed back outside. Aunt Jane and Uncle Nick were already fighting the flames with bed sheets and buckets of water. Evidently, they must have smelt the flames and gone outside while Ann was looking inside.

Pam had started moving the horses out through the back door. Ann wondered if she might help in some way. Pam gently but quickly was leading out Jewel. Swiftly, she led him into a fenced in pen where Daylight and Crystal already stood.

"Can I help?" Ann asked. She swiftly followed Pam into the burning barn. Pam urged Ivy forward, away from the flames. He still limped from his broken leg. Pam led him out the door. Ann looked around wildly. There was only one horse left, *Black Mystery!*

The black horse reared up in fright. Flames leapt towards his stall. Ann must do something quick! Dodging flames and coughing for air, Ann made it to the stall. Unlatching the door quickly, Ann bravely led the circus horse out.

"Come on, boy! Come on!" The horse was frightened and would not go on. Ann remembered reading somewhere that if a horse could not see danger, he would trust you more. Quickly, Ann tied a bandana that she snatched off the wall over Black Mystery's eyes. Together they made it out into the fresh air. Ann was coughing violently. Pam ran and hugged her. "Thank goodness you're safe!" she cried. They put Black Mystery in the pen and Pam undid the bandana.

Aunt Jane and Uncle Nick now had the fire under control. Soon it died down all together. The barn was just a heap of smothering ruins. Uncle Nick wearily sat down to rest. "Are all the horses safe, Pam?"

"Yes, dad," came the quiet response. Then more energetically she said, "Ann risked her life to save Black Mystery!" Pam praised her brave cousin. Uncle Nick smiled at Ann.

"I only did it for Dick. I promised him that I wouldn't let Mystery be taken away," Ann said quietly.

"At least the fire didn't touch the house." Aunt Jane looked on the bright side.

"Yes, and I'll have a new barn built in this one's place." Uncle Nick agreed.

"Any idea how the fire got started?" Ann asked.

"No, I don't," Uncle Nick said.

They all went inside for lunch for they were starved and exhausted. The next day, Uncle Nick had a company take away all the barn debris and begin building a new barn. Black Mystery's leg was entirely healed, the only trace of the injuries existence was a faint scar. Uncle Nick said this would be gone by the competition. Ann was glad. How pleased Dick would be!

Ann wanted to start training Black Mystery, but she wondered what he would do. The people at the circus didn't want him because he was too crazy. Ann wondered if Black Mystery would just buck her off.

First Pam helped Ann put the halter on Mystery. He didn't seem to mind this. Ann led him around to become more acquainted to it. Then she groomed him. He seemed to enjoy the attention. And although Mystery did not mind being led or groomed, he was not very fond of the other horses. Sometimes, he tried to bite or kick them. They kept him away from them in his own pasture area.

81

Before Ann knew it, it was Saturday. She decided to give Dick a call, hoping he wouldn't be in the middle of an activity. To her luck Dick answered the phone.

"Hello, how is everything?"Dick inquired.

"Hi, Dick!" Ann greeted him warmly. "Everything is awesome! Guess what?! Black Mystery isn't really wild. He's a run-away from the circus!" Ann was brimming with news.

"What? How do you know?"

"It was on the front page of the newspaper! And they don't even really want him back because he was kind of crazy. So, we are keeping him!"

" Cool! Wish I could be there," said Dick.

"Well..." Ann then continued, "His leg is all better. I've done some leading and grooming with him. Only one problem, he isn't too fond of the others."

"In what way?" Dick asked over the phone.

"He sometimes tries to bite or kick the other horses."

"Does he do that to people?"

"Not really, he seems pretty calm around us."

"Have you tried riding him yet?"

"I haven't at all." Ann was sorry to disappoint her cousin. "Fact is," she continued, "I'm a little afraid to try."

"Oh?"

"Yeah, but maybe I'll try today. Oh, and something else happened: the barn burnt down! Nobody knows the reason why. At least all the horses are safe."

"What! That *is* a surprise."

They talked a little longer; Dick told of some of the adventures he'd had at camp. Then, Dick had to go, so they hung up. Ann went outside to the pen. Workmen still hammered away on the barn. Ann opened the pen door, quickly closing it behind her. Pam was already in there. She was unsaddling Lilac.

"Hi, Ann. I just got back from a trail ride, what are you up to?"

"Not sure... I thought I'd try riding Mystery. Guess I would like some help. What saddle do you think would work for him?"

"Maybe Daylight's. I can help you if you like. I'm finished here." Pam came over.

They went out to a different pen where Black Mystery was all by himself. They approached the horse and put on a halter. Pam strapped on Daylight's saddle, making sure everything was right. She took off the halter and put on reins.

Mystery followed Pam as she led him out. "I'm gonna bring him over there."

"Okay. I just want to see if I can ride him at all." Ann didn't feel very confident. At the mounting block, Ann climbed the stairs. Taking a deep breath she inserted one foot in a stirrup. Swinging her leg over, she put it in the other stirrup. She sat down. Suddenly, Black Mystery reared up on his hind legs!

Chapter Fourteen: The Horse Money

Ann held on for dear life. She grasped the strong arched neck. Mystery galloped away into the woods. He raced by trees and whizzed by low branches. They kept whacking Ann's face and she was scared. The black horse was going incredibly fast!

Trying to slow the galloping horse, inexperienced Ann pulled hard on the reins shouting, "Whoa boy! Stop!" Ann shouted this again and again. It only seemed to make him run faster. What would Ann do?

Everything seemed a blur as Mystery raced on. All Ann wanted to do was get down safely!

"Oh, please boy, stop. I'm so scared!"

Mystery breathed heavily to keep up his neck breaking speed. Ann pulled the reins sharply to the left. If she couldn't get him to stop, maybe he would turn around. Pam could help her!

Amazingly, the black racer obeyed. Turning in a wide circle, the duo trotted back to the farm. "Good boy," Ann breathed, petting the sweaty neck. Pam hurried to the runaway horse and led him to the mounting block to let Ann climb down. She did this quite willingly! "Enough riding for today," panted Ann who was still recovering from the excitement.

"I agree. Perhaps, we need to do more ground work and ride in a fenced in area. I could ride as well. You handled the situation well, though!" Pam praised the younger girl.

"Thanks," Ann half smiled; at least something was good.

Pam groomed Black Mystery and took off the riding equipment. Ann decided to check on her little bunny. She found the cage and crouched down. Putting her fingers between the wire she patted Clover's head. "How ya doin?" Ann was proud of her little rabbit. Clover's tiny bright eyes looked up. She hopped to the other side of the cage. Ann thought she was adorable. Her thoughts drifted to the upcoming horse competition. She felt rather nervous about the whole thing. She wished Dick was there. She missed her adventurous cousin. Pam was ok, but she lacked the enthusiasm and humor of her younger brother. How would everything go? Ann was so unsure.

Suddenly she became aware of a someone standing behind her.

Is it Uncle Nick? Ann wondered as she turned her head. It was a tall skinny man with blond hair who seemed to be in his thirties. At first sight, Ann thought he was one of the men working on the barn, but when he spoke, Ann knew otherwise…

"Hello, my name is Mr. Woodland. Is your father home? I've come to speak to him regarding the circus horse, Midnight." Ann was alarmed and at once stood up.

"Ah…yes, my Uncle Nick is here, is that who you mean? I think he's in the house… I'll get him."

"Thank you. Yes, please do."

Ann raced inside, her heart throbbing. What was this about the circus horse? His real name was Midnight?! Would they take him away? Oh no, Ann could not let him go, for

Dick's sake. He was rather wild, yet he just needed a little work!

Uncle Nick was soon told the news and came out to meet the young man. Ann was too afraid of what would be said so she went inside. Oh, what would happen? Ann waited a while, and ate a snack with Pam. There were grapes, crackers, and cheese that Aunt Jane had prepared if anyone got hungry. Ann explained to Pam about the man that Uncle Nick had gone to talk to.

"Maybe he just wants to look him over and make sure he's ok," Pam thought up an idea.

"I don't know. He sounded rather serious," Ann replied. She then introduced her worry. "What if they want him back?"

"They said we could keep him… it's… it's unlikely that they want him back."

"But still," Ann persisted.

"I suppose," Pam sighed as she bit into a grape.

Oh, Dick will be so mad if they take Black Mystery! Please don't! And not just that, I think that I like him too. Although he is wildish, it makes him all the more strong and fit for the competition. Ann pleaded silently. Somehow, she too had fallen in love with the black beauty!

At last after about half an hour, Uncle Nick came into the kitchen with Aunt Jane. "Well, children," he addressed the girls. "This is how it is." Ann took a deep breath awaiting and expecting the worst. "Mr. Woodland, he wants us to pay for that horse. We can keep him if we pay."

How much?" ventured Pam. Ann was too frightened to speak.

"They want about two thousand dollars."

Pam seemed startled. "That much?"

"Yes, dear. Mr. Woodland told me they put a lot of money into that horse and since it turned out to be a failure…"

To Ann, Uncle Nick's voice stopped as she caught those last words: "Turned out to be a failure." *A failure! No, Black Mystery wasn't a failure! They were wrong. Just because he needed help with taming… well, it didn't mean he was a failure! How cruel!* And yet, Ann realized it definitely was hard to ride him. But how could they have no patience?

"What do you think, Ann?" Pam questioned.
"About what?" Ann hadn't really been paying attention to the conversation.
"About the money? Would you really want to trade a different horse for the new one?"
Ann was sorry she hadn't been paying attention. She wished she had. "Oh, ah… I don't exactly understand."
"Well, the only way we can pay the two thousand dollars, is to sell a different horse. It might not make two thousand, but it certainly would help," was Uncle Nick's statement.
"Oh?" Ann was surprised and her mind raced to think of what horse they would sell. "Couldn't we just pay without selling a horse?" Ann asked when she couldn't bear to sell any of them.
"Sorry, Ann, I don't have that kind of money."

Ann didn't want this to happen! *What could work? How would they do it?* "Maybe Jewel?" Ann mentioned the horse she was the least attached to.
"Well it might not bring such a good price as a younger horse," Aunt Jane spoke wisely.
"Perhaps the black horse isn't such a good idea after all," Uncle Nick continued. "We are rather tight with money and the barn burning down and all."

"Oh please, I think we can do it!" Ann pleaded much to their surprise.

"To think how much you've changed," Aunt Jane sighed.

Ann went to bed that night feeling depressed at the prospect which lay before them. She knew that they *had* to keep Black Mystery, and yet, how?

Ann awoke to a beautiful Sunday morning. A bar of golden light streamed in from the large window at the opposite side of the cute bedroom. The family did their chores and washed up to go to church. Ann couldn't wait till Dick was home, only tomorrow! After church and a yummy lunch of fried chicken and salad, Ann and Pam continued their training. They had only six days before the big day!

Autumn was doing great, but would Black Mystery be ready? Ann didn't know. Pam saddled Mystery up, ready to try again. She talked soothingly to him so he would be calm. Ann held the rope so he couldn't bolt off. She hoped she was strong enough to hold him. Pam was going to ride.

Uncle Nick had decided to sell Jewel and Crystal. They now could keep Black Mystery. What a relief for Ann! It was sad and yet at least *he* was truly theirs!

Pam climbed into the saddle. Mystery took a small step forward. Ann hoped he would be better, perhaps their extra training would help, but who knew?

Chapter Fifteen: Gone

The black horse was definitely skittish, unsure, and scared. Pam seemed very confident, though maybe her looks were deceiving. "Come on, boy..." Ann's cousin would just stay inside the fenced-in area, a field next to the in-process new barn. Mystery seemed better now that they were in the outside arena. Ann stopped leading and now stepped aside to watch the action, if anything would come of it. Pam led him into a trot, canter, everything was going so well! Finally, he had earned their trust. Dick would be happy!

Ann still wondered how the fire started, since they found no evidence. But how could this be? Ann could tell, when on the phone with Dick, that he was worried about all the excitement going on at home. Black Mystery was doing great, and after an hour or so, Pam dismounted.

"He's doing so well!" Pam smiled as she pat Mystery's warm neck.

"Pam, how do you think the fire started?" Ann wondered if it could happen again, maybe this time to the house?

"Maybe a lantern wasn't put out. Or maybe someone did it purposely? I don't really know."

Ann didn't like to think about the latter response, who would do such a thing?

Going inside, Pam and Ann found Uncle Nick on the phone, apparently with the police. They seemed to be concerned that maybe there was something dangerous to the family that caused the fire. They were sending someone to look at it right away. Ann was worried about the outcome. She told

Pam they needed to work on Autumn. They had less than a week, and the competition awaited!

A police car came up the dirt road. The whole family was present to greet the policeman. "Afternoon!" the muscular man said politely. Then he turned his attention to the remains of the burnt-down barn.

It was 1:30 p.m. Pam took Ann to saddle up Autumn. Riding inside the fence, Ann felt like her whole world had changed. Her whole perspective on horses and her summer was entirely different. Pam was giving riding tips. Ann thought about how on Saturday they would decorate the horses. Ann especially thought about combing their hair, making it shiny, just like new!

The policeman looked very intrigued, Ann thought as she glanced over. She could hear bits and pieces of conversation coming from the burned barn. "You say it was 'bout evening?" The authority eyed his surroundings. He continued, "Do you know anyone who would do such a thing? Maybe there was a lit lantern?" He began again to look around, after getting all the facts and answers that were known.

Autumn was sapped out of energy, so was Ann. So she put the horse back in the strong pen. Then Ann went to where the rest of the family was. As she did so, the policeman just stepped back into his bright lighted car. The cousins went to see what the man had thought of the situation.

"What did he say, Dad?" Pam crossed her arms and awaited an answer.

"After all the answers we gave him, he said maybe it was purposeful. He took samples to find fingerprints." Ann got tense by this response.

All of them, without saying much at all, went inside for the cookies Aunt Jane would have ready soon. After cookies, Ann went outside to play with Clover. She found that trying to teach bunny tricks is super hard!

Time seemed to go by fast. Dick would be home next morning. Uncle Nick would pick him up at ten-thirty. Ann was very excited. The phone rang just then. Uncle Nick answered it.

"Hello?" He answered, hoping for a believable answer from the police.

"Yes, this is the sheriff's department, we are calling to inform you we have found some fingerprints here… on some of the unburned fragments. We have proof here, unless you know the owner of these prints. See here, we seem to believe they are the fingerprints of Caleb Sanders. He has had incidents like this before, it seems to be purposeful…"

"Hold on, sir…" Uncle Nick said quickly, yet thinking slowly to the back of his memory. "I know, I know that name!"

"Has he done anything to you or your property before?" asked the voice on the other end.

"Not specifically to me, but to someone else!"

"Please explain," said the sheriff's department. The officer reached for a paper and pen.

"Caleb Sanders was an enemy of my father… I haven't seen him for years… when I did, he always seemed to be mad about something my Dad did. How my Dad had owned the yellow farmhouse down the road a mile or so. And now that my father has passed away, we own it. Many things happened in the past, but continue mildly in the future. He wanted that farm, he didn't have enough to pay for it though. He was destructive in various ways. And many examples show it!"

Uncle Nick continued thinking about the main problem. Caleb had probably set fire to the barn. If Pam and Ann weren't there, the house could have gone up in flames along with it!

The policeman took a deep breath and sighed. "But why, after all these years?" asked the authority.

"Maybe he's in a desperate situation..." Uncle Nick questioned himself, trying to think of a more specific answer. But he didn't have any more proof.

Morning came, and with it, Dick. Ann ran up to him as the car pulled through the dusty driveway. "Dick!" She was eager to tell her cousin about the happenings during the time he was gone. Dick and Ann were excited to get back to training. Ann felt happy and proud because at least she *tried* riding Mystery. Pam was the one who had done it successfully, though. Ann decided to tell Dick about the horses they had to sell.

Dick took his cousin outside after lunch, to work on stuff for the competition. "How's Mystery?" said an excited Dick, when he had hurried to the beautiful penned in horse. "Hey boy!" he stroked the dark face.

Ann showed Dick the things she had learned. An impressed look came upon his face as the girl got down from Autumn's high back. "You're amazing!" he complimented. Surprised, yet hopeful, Dick got on Mystery. He was ready to ride, or was he?

Dick knew how fast and beautiful the horse was. What about jumping fences though? Dick decided to try that. He set up some barrels to work around and fences that reached at least as high as Ann's ribs. To Ann the moment felt slow-motion. Was it the same for Dick? A solemn look came across his tanned face, his shoulders were in a perfectly relaxed position, but was his trust in perfect position also?

The form of the horse swept beautifully over the wooden poles. Ann exchanged looks with Dick. Dick and Mystery were ready, but was Ann? She got on Autumn. She was going to try jumping. She would try to learn from Dick. She prepared herself.

"Now remember what I told you!" the boy cousin called.

"I know... confidence is key!" a smile traced her precipitated face. She was ready! Autumn was, next to Mystery, the best jumper there. It definitely showed as they passed gracefully over!

"I can't believe it!" Ann yelled across the field, "I did it!" Dick raced Mystery across the tall hills where he once freely roamed. Ann followed, her hair blowing in the wind. The happy moments stopped then, as a car near where the cousins were riding slowly started to roll away, then faster. Ann's eyes looked to Dick's. Something felt wrong, something *was* wrong.

Back at home, Uncle Nick listened quietly on the phone as the police had located their man, Caleb. "4367 Woodland Inn," said the sheriff. "We'll pay a visit to him as soon as we hang..." The last words of the officer were cut off. The phone line and power had been disconnected.

"What happened?" Uncle Nick shouted, as Dick and Ann both entered the suddenly darkened room, very surprised.

"There's no storm." Dick would know, having just been outside.

"I, uh, did see someone in a tinted car by the telephone and electricity pole... if that means anything..." Ann's voice trailed off, as did her train of thought.

"Caleb." Uncle Nick said this one word as if it were final. Then he went outside to see if he could fix the problem. Yet the problem he could not fix was in the heart of Caleb Sanders.

Uncle Nick, having some knowledge and experience as an electrician, was able to get the power back on. Pam and Ann enjoyed the light, as they planned out how they would do the horses hair and decorations. Saturday was coming with great speed; they had very little time.

Dinner was being made by Aunt Jane. Dick and Ann planned to go on a trail ride after dinner. The police arrived at the found apartment address, as the family back at the house was enjoying the very good cooking. Uncle Nick was at home with them, but his mind was mostly on what the police would figure out.

There was nothing Ann and Dick could do to help the problem, so as soon as they finished, they went to go on their prearranged trail ride. They went out to the field where the pen was.

"Autumn! Autumn!" Ann called.

Both of the cousins turned tense and frightened. The two cousins burst through the front door startling the rest of the family. "Autumn... it's Autumn..." Ann began breathlessly.

Dick couldn't manage not having a say:

"Autumn's gone!" his boyish voice echoed on the walls. Silence followed. Then slowly, Dick's father rose out of his seat and dialed the police:

"Caleb, he's struck again!"

Chapter Sixteen: Caleb's Story

Ann sunk down to the floor and sobbed. "Oh, honey," Aunt Jane tried to comfort her young niece. "We'll get her back."

"But… but what will… will that terrible man d...do to her?" Ann stammered. But Aunt Jane could offer no response.

Dick paced the floor. What had been going on while he was away? Who was this Caleb guy? He had no right to set fire to the barn, turn off the power, and steal Autumn! Dick wasn't mad, he was *furious!* He pounded his fist into the back of a chair.

Uncle Nick hung up on the phone with the police. "What did they say?" Dick and Pam asked in unison. Ann looked up at Uncle Nick's tense face. He sighed deeply before answering:

"They talked to Caleb at the inn where he is currently staying. Yet, it seems he denies having any knowledge of the fire in the barn or power outage. As for the horse, he also lied that he did not know of its disappearance…"

"That devil of a man!" interrupted Dick.

"Hold your tongue, young man." Aunt Jane spoke bitterly.

"Yes, Mom." But inside, Dick's anger could not quench itself.

Uncle Nick continued, "The police don't think there's enough evidence. Just my word against his."

"But the fingerprints… and the car," Aunt Jane broke in.

"They think..." Uncle Nick began, but said no more.

"Think *what?*" his worried wife questioned.

"Oh, never mind! It's gone too far, this whole thing has gone *too far*!" Uncle Nick's words lashed out at his wife.

Ann, who still was a huddled figure on the floor, began to think. And her thoughts began to race. *Autumn... she's my favorite! The very thought of what that man might do...* Ann was exhausted and dozed off right there on the floor.

It was a while later when Ann awoke. Tuesday morning was here. She was lying in her bed. *Uncle Nick must've led me up,* Ann thought. Her thoughts once again drifted to Autumn. She tried to put it out of her mind, but she could not. Ann slowly dressed. Then went down for breakfast.

Everyone was up. The table was quiet except the clatter of plates. They were eating blueberry pancakes. Ann ate in silence. After the strange breakfast and clean-up, Ann and Dick went outside. They began to clean some of the horse fertilizer in the pens.

"Hi, boy." Ann patted Black Mystery's sleek neck. She saw something moving out of the corner of her eye. She turned. Ann hardly dared to breathe. Was she just imagining?

"What's up, Ann?" Dick noticed her sudden stillness.

"I... I saw her, Dick! She was there just a minute ago!"

"What? Who?"

"Autumn."

"Are you crazy?!"

"No Dick. She was really there! Believe me. She was just coming out of the bushes then stopped and ran off! Dick, oh Dick, is it possible that somehow Autumn could have got out of the pen? And... and got lost and I saw her, right?"

"It's so unlikely..."

"Come on, Dick! Might be our only chance!"

The cousins sprinted into the woods. Dick had a hunch that Ann was wrong, but then again, he was beginning to doubt everything. The woods were still dim; it was early morning. The grass was wet and dewy against their bare legs.

"Autumn, Autumn..." Ann called softly. She knew loud noises would scare the poor horse. She then heard a low whinny. Ann was right!

"She must be around here!" Dick was excited. Autumn's familiar figure emerged from the trees. Ann raced up to the horse and hugged it.

"I'm so glad you're safe!" Ann cried.

"But I don't understand," Dick said. "Autumn could not have gotten out of the pen. And I thought Caleb took her..."

"Well, we don't know that for sure. Maybe she escaped from that man!"

They lead the horse back to the pen and latched it.

"Let's tell Dad!" said Dick. Uncle Nick would not believe them until he saw for himself.

"I still think Caleb is behind this," he grumbled.

"Nick," Aunt Jane said as she came out of the house, "You're wanted on the phone, it's the police."

Uncle Nick hurried inside, Ann and Dick followed. Uncle Nick was on the phone for about ten minutes. Then he hung up and started putting on his shoes.

"Where are you going?" Dick asked his father.

"I can't explain, it's urgent son." Uncle Nick hurried off. He was gone almost all of the day. During the day, Dick, Pam, and Ann trained on their horses some more. They also went on a trail ride.

"Where've you been, Nick?" Aunt Jane asked at dinner.

"That's a long story," was the short response.

"Tell us, Dad," Dick said impatiently.

"Well," Uncle Nick began, and then continued: "When the police called they told me Caleb got in a car accident on the highway. He was injured badly and the chance of survival for him was slim. He told the doctor at the hospital that he had to tell me something before he died. So, I went."

"What did he say?" asked Aunt Jane.

"He told me that he did put the fire to the barn and messed with the lights. As for Autumn, he led her out of the pen and into the woods hoping she'd never find her way back."

"But why?" Pam questioned. "Why did he do it?"

"He had long held a grudge against my father. He offered a fair sum of money for this place but my father refused him, giving the property to me, his son. Caleb was a proud and wealthy man. He planned to enter his own horse into that competition. But he knew that Dick, here, had a fine chance of winning. He set fire to the barn in hope of killing your horse so he could win the competition."

"He was willing to kill us, all just for money?" Dick asked confused.

"He was a greedy and selfish man," Uncle Nick stated solemnly.

"*Was?*" Pam asked.

"He died while I was there," her father explained.

"Oh," said Pam quietly.

"I still don't quite understand," said Dick thoughtfully. "Why'd he mess with the lights? And it still doesn't explain letting Autumn loose."

"Well, after learning that we survived the fire and all the horses were still safe, Caleb was still very determined. He did those things to try and frighten you from entering. Nothing could please him more than to get back at my father, even if it was by hurting us."

"But why bother telling you it all?" Aunt Jane wondered aloud.

"He knew his death was nearing. I guess it was on his mind and troubled him. By confessing to me, maybe it eased his conscience," was his answer.

Silence now fell. Ann silently prayed for the dead man's soul. And now that all the trouble with Caleb was over, everyone felt much safer.

Saturday crept forward slowly. Ann felt she was ready for the competition. She was very excited. It was also good that Black Mystery was adjusting to other horses and forgetting his old biting and kicking habits.

Ann got on Autumn. She must train whenever she could. She was going to make everyone proud. Very proud. They raced across the field together in a fast canter. They were like one, all their movements blending into each other. Then as if they were a bird, they glided over the fence in astounding unity, speed, and beauty.

"You're amazing!" Dick complemented once again, as he trailed behind on the "wild horse."

Blushing, Ann replied, "Everything I know came from you."

"Not everything," Dick corrected. "I think you were just born to ride horses. I was not so great as you when I started."

They jumped the fence once more. As Autumn trotted back to the barn, Ann looked up at the late Thursday morning sky. "Lunch should be soon," Ann thought happily. She was starved. And the food at Blueberry Ridge was always delicious. Ann and Dick dismounted.

"Let's groom them, they're kinda dirty," Dick suggested.

"Sure." Ann began to go in circles with a soft brush on Autumn's sides. Dick did the same to his horse.

While they groomed, the cousins talked:

"On Saturday morning, we're gonna wash the horses. Make them all clean. Besides, they like cooling off. Then we'll brush 'em and groom them, make them all pretty," Dick informed her.

"Is the beauty contest first, then?" Ann wanted to know.

"Uh-huh. They pick the nicest-looking horse... and, of course, you get ribbons and stuff. Then there's the race. You get one hundred dollars if you win. Then the trophy goes to the best jumper."

"Neat!" Ann was thrilled. As an afterthought she added: "If you only get ribbons and trophies, or like a hundred bucks, why did Caleb want to win so badly?"

"I don't know. Guess it was mostly for pride."

Dick and Ann put the groomed horses in the new barn. Then they went inside. "You're just in time for lunch," Aunt Jane said. "There's bacon, lettuce, and tomato sandwiches, along with fruit, chips, and carrot sticks. Oh, and here, Ann. You can take these carrot peels to Clover."

"Thank you."

Ann went outside and fed her cute little baby bunny the carrot scraps. Clover began to eat them. Ann pet her soft brown fur. Wiggling her pink nose, Clover blinked her tiny black eyes. "Bye, sweety," Ann told her pet.

Back in the house they said grace and began eating their luncheon. "You know, Dad, Ann's gotten to be an expert rider. She just might beat me in the competition." Dick sounded serious.

Ann laughed. "I have learned a considerable lot, but I'm certainly not an expert."

"Do you think you're ready?" her uncle asked.

"Sure," Ann shrugged. Although Ann pretended to be casual, she was rather uptight about it all. Dick was always complimenting her, but was she as good as all that?

A sudden knock on the door startled those seated. Who could it be and what would they want? Uncle Nick slowly rose to answer the unexpected visitor's call...

Chapter Seventeen: The Long-awaited Contest

Slowly the door creaked open. An elderly lady wearing a soft pink dress stepped into the front room. Dick's mouth dropped open in disbelief. "Grandma!" he nearly shouted.

"What a surprise!" Uncle Nick cried, hugging his mother.

"Oh, dear, goodness me! I did call to tell you I was coming didn't I? Well, actually, maybe I didn't. Hmmm... I can't remember!" she laughed.

Aunt Jane displayed a secret smile and winked. "I thought it would be a good surprise for the family," she said.

"You knew all along?" smiled Pam, figuring it out.

Ann was a little nervous. She had never met Dick's grandma before. She was Uncle Nick's mother so Ann was not related. Aunt Jane and Ann's mother were the related ones.

The family gathered around Dick and Pam's grandma. Ann soon found out that her name was Margaret. They all tried to make her feel at home. She joined them for lunch and they talked for a while. They asked her if she had a nice trip and all that.

Dick brought up the horse competition when he felt it appropriate. "Good for you!" replied the old woman with energy. "Your grandpa would be so proud of you!"

"Yes, he would," Dick agreed.

"We're entering Autumn and Black Mystery," Ann informed Grandma Margaret.

"Oh?" she questioned, "You have a new horse?" She turned to Uncle Nick.

"Oh, yes," he answered, adding, "it's a long story. I'll tell you some time, but now, I think it is time for..." he motioned towards the kitchen. All eyes turned and saw Aunt Jane coming in with a beautiful blueberry cobbler. She had just gotten it out of the oven.

And so they all ate a hearty dessert. Everyone thought it was delicious. Grandma was going to stay for awhile. She wanted to "watch Dick win the competition," as she put it. Ann thought she was a very nice lady and made up her mind to get to know her better.

They all helped Grandma set up in the guest bedroom. Soon she was settled. Dick and Ann wanted to show her the horses, but Aunt Jane said that they shouldn't pressure and hurry her too much.

"No, it's perfectly fine. I'd love to see your horses. I would have one myself except I can't ride very well anymore. I'm not so active as I use to be."

Grandma put on her shoes, and Dick and Ann strapped riding boots on their feet. The trio walked briskly to the barn. Dick began to tell his grandma about their discovery of Mystery. She seemed very interested. He began: "We found Black Mystery in an adventurous ride on the trails. Then late one night, during a storm, my father helped me bring him here, since he was hurt..."

Ann continued Dick's drama, "Originally we thought that he was a wild horse because of Dick's stories of your husband. But later we found out that he was actually a run-away from the circus. We loved him so much that we sold Crystal and Jewel for money to give to the circus so we could keep him. The circus really didn't want him anyway. He was rather untamed. But we've gentled him, and now he's almost perfect!"

"Really? What a story!" Grandma sounded amazed.

They opened the door and entered the barn. "This is Daylight, you may remember him from before."

"Yes, I do," Grandma stroked Daylight's forehead.

"I was wondering," Ann began as they continued down the aisle, "if any other horses here were from Dick's grandfather. I mean to say that we found out that he saved Autumn when she was a baby. So maybe some of the others are saved wild horses." Ann tried to explain.

"Well now," Grandma started, "I remember there was a horse..." she stopped a moment, trying to remember so long ago. She began again, "He was dark gray and spotted white. We might have given him to your father, Dick. I think we called him June."

"Oh, you mean Jewel?" questioned Dick.

"We sold that horse." Ann stated, now feeling rather guilty that they had.

"No, as I remember Jewel had a twin sister Crystal, right?"

"Yes."

"No, this was a different horse. I think he was actually more of a pony..."

Dick and Ann wondered about the horse or pony Grandma was talking about.

"Perhaps, he's still here?" Grandma asked.

"No... I never knew of such a horse..." Dick replied.

"That's a pity. I rather liked him."

"Is it possible that you gave the pony, June, to someone else?" Ann suggested.

"Maybe we did. I can't remember. It *was* so long ago..."

Presently they came to Black Mystery's stall. They fed him some carrots that Ann had brought. "He is a beautiful horse," Grandma remarked. The black horse crunched the thick orange carrot that Ann held out to him.

"What happened here?" Grandma questioned when they got to Ivy's stall. Dick explained the tragic fall, and how his horse was still recovering. Lilac and Autumn were shown as well. They talked some more and then went back inside. Pam fell to showing Grandma her new recipes she had learned. "See here, you mix the butter and sugar together, then add the flour mixture…" their conversation dragged on.

Seeing as Dick and Ann weren't so interested, they went to do something more exciting: chores. Ann headed out for the barn again. She thought about the old barn and imagined the fire. It had been so frightening. But she shook the thought out of her mind. Her boots brushed past the rather long grass on her way. Then she changed her mind and went to look at the pigs. Ann hadn't really seen them the whole time she'd been there. Their pen was muddy and smelly. There were four black and white pigs who grunted as they greedily fought over drinking and eating. Ann watched them amused for a few minutes. She decided to fill up their water since it was low. Ann then spent the rest of the day visiting with the goats, ducklings, and cows that there had not been much time to see before. She had been so excited about horses that she almost completely forgot about them.

Time passed quickly and soon it was Saturday morning. Ann was so excited she felt she would burst. Bright and early the whole family was awake. After a quick breakfast, although Ann and Dick could hardly eat, they skipped out to the barn once more. The grass was wet with dew. The sun was just rising and sparkled on the water droplets, in a rainbow of color. A bird burst into song. Ann could hardly contain her anxiousness.

Unlatching the big door Dick and Ann went in. They walked over to Autumn and Black Mystery. Ann had learned how to put the halter on. She slipped it over Autumn's head. She knotted it as she whispered in Autumns ear: "You're going to do fine, right girl? Make us proud. I love you." She pat Autumn's forehead as she looked into her deep dark eyes. "Ok. Let's get you all prettied up!"

The cousins washed, brushed, and braided the horses. Ann took special care of it this time, trying not to miss a spot! Uncle Nick and Aunt Jane were trying to hook up the horse trailer. It was a little difficult, but they succeeded. "Pam, did you pack the lunches?" Aunt Jane was asking her daughter.

"Yeah, they're on the kitchen table in a cooler with water bottles."

"Great. You should put some hay and apples, maybe even some horse treats in the trailer. Put in the riding equipment too," Aunt Jane set her daughter to work.

"Ok." Pam dutifully fulfilled her mother's request.

Before she knew it, Ann was leading Autumn into the trailer. Autumn's big hooves make a clip-clop as she nervously walked up the ramp. "Alright, Dick. Bring Mystery in," she called. Black Mystery was hesitant and resisted.

"Come on boy, it's all right. This is our big day. We can't do this without you," Dick tugged on the rope. Mystery backed off, fearing the trailer with wild eyes. Uncle Nick came to give his son a hand. He gave Mystery a slight slap on the back and yelled a little.

"Sometimes you gotta use a little force," he grinned as the black horse trotted in. The eager family closed the trailer door and climbed into their truck. Uncle Nick had sold the car for the used truck and he seemed to like the exchange. Uncle Nick started up the truck and turned out of the yard onto the road. He continued driving.

"Where's your grandma?" Ann questioned. She hadn't seen the old lady since last night.

Dick answered her, "She'll be coming shortly. We have to be there early."

"Aren't you excited?" Ann asked Dick, her own excitement bubbling inside her. She was rather jumpy.

"Excited? I'm not just excited! I'm extremely excited! And oh, Ann, by the way, I forgot to tell you that ah, whatever you do, don't ever, *ever*...."

"What? Don't ever what?"

"Lose!" Dick laughed and Ann joined in. They were in good spirits and very happy.

The old truck rattled into the place where the competitions were to take place. Ann saw many people and horses. It was almost overwhelming. Uncle Nick parked. Dick was the first to jump out, Ann following close behind.

They all went to sign in and fill out some registration forms. Soon, they were shown the temporary stable they'd keep the horses in between contests. Autumn and Mystery were led in.

Uncle Nick glanced at his watch, they had five minutes to spare; the time dragged on endlessly for Ann. Finally all the contestants lined up. The judges examined the horses. Ann studied the horses critically. She looked back at Autumn. Who

was the prettiest? A judge stopped in front of Autumn. Ann
held her breath.

Chapter Eighteen: Across the Finish Line

Dick was next to Ann, they exchanged nervous looks, and both anticipating the results. "Very nice!" The judge wrote something on his clipboard. The judge then looked over Black Mystery, they both looked amazing!

There were ten contestants including the cousins. Pam and the rest of the family watched eagerly behind a white fence. After examining them all, the judge stepped up to the podium. Ann prayed in hopes of her victory, and Dick silently did the same.

"Do they announce each competition after each one? Or after it all?" Ann asked nervously.

"Yeah, after each one." Dick answered a bit distracted; he was watching the judge intently.

"Thank you all for coming out today!" The judge began, "I am pleased to announce a tie…"

Ann's heart skipped a beat. Ann wondered as she looked at the other competitors; hers and Dick's were definitely the best. Right?

The judge finished his sentence, "Autumn entered by Ann Melonwood, and Black Mystery, entered by Dick Preston!"

The cousins were glad, and joined in the clapping which heavily echoed from the crowd. "Now we just have to nail the other two competitions!" Dick encouraged. Ann nodded, congratulating her cousin. Next was the race!

"Take your mark!" A voice called loudly from a microphone up in the stands.

"Ready, Ann?" asked Dick, getting in position.

"Ready." Ann concentrated on the track; two laps would end the race. The horn blew and the racers sped across the starting line. The family watched intently, taking pictures and videos. Ann was presently in third.

Black Mystery was known for speed. Ann was speeding up. The competitor in second fell after slipping on mud, which was put in the track as an obstacle. Ann learning as she went, dodged the sabotage and was in second.

One more lap to go… the others were behind, they didn't treat their horses as well. They yelled and slapped them rudely. Ann and Dick encouraged with kind words, and if needed, tightened their knees softly to hurry the animal.

With only half a lap to go, Ann was going so fast, she felt the urge to slow down. But slowing down would not win the competition! Dick looked very concentrated. Ann couldn't stay solemn, "Come on girl, I believe in you."

Memories of her time at Blueberry Ridge flashed through her mind. She would be leaving that Monday. Time had gone by so fast. Dick continued in first place, Ann stayed close behind. She sped up as much as Autumn could bear. They passed the finish line, Ann taking second place, Dick in first. Afterwards, both dismounted, hugging each other in congratulations.

"You were amazing!" Another compliment eased Ann's worry.

"So were you. First place in wonderful!" she returned the compliment.

"Next is jumping…" Dick said, "Autumn is best known for that!"

Ann hadn't practiced jumping as much as racing, a hint of regret tinted her mind. "Don't worry, Ann!" Dick comforted. "She's got this."

Ann trusted his words, trying to relax. They had five minutes before the first competitor would start.

They went, one by one. Dick was next in line. The fences were high, and Ann, known for worry, hoped she wouldn't fall off, but she had done this before. She needed to trust. "Trust." She echoed in a louder whisper, "Trust!"

The other competitors did well, but harshness didn't help. It was Dick's turn, and he mounted as they called his name. He gave a reassuring nod to Ann who bit her lip: she was next.

Black Mystery looked determined, his rider seemed ready too. "You've got this, boy!" he encouraged, getting a whinny for Mystery's response. Dick easily made it over the first jump, but there were seven more. The hedges were next. He brushed up a little bit but nothing worth losing for, or was it? Ann wondered about this, not exactly knowing the rules that guided the rider and the horse. Dick hit softly on the last one, but he didn't think the judges saw. Mystery had been a little hesitant though.

Applause filled the summer air as Dick dismounted. He hugged Ann, as she mounted. "I'm ready, ok, I can do this!" She had come so far… she came to Blueberry Ridge, terrified at the thought of horses. Look where she was now! Her parents would be so proud.

She was off, Autumn was an expert and Ann became one with the horse in motion. With ease, Autumn dodged the bars and hedges. Autumn skidded a bit but completed the course in a commendable amount of time. Ann was so proud. "We did it!" She called. "We did it..."

The announcement exclaimed Ann as the winner; Dick got third. The second place didn't much mess up but took more time. Uncle Nick and Aunt Jane celebrated from their spot behind the fence.

The videos and pictures would be so fun to watch and look at! The competition was over, and two exhausted cousins, after receiving their prizes, got into the humid truck. Grandma Margaret followed in her own car.

The cousins wondered about the gray and white pony. Ann remembered that Dick brought up once his embarrassing encounter when he first started riding. She would ask him when they got home. She was even more eager to know.

Ann's parents would pick Ann up on Monday morning. It was only two days away! At least she would keep the bunny, Clover. "We have plenty of videos and pictures," said Uncle Nick, as if that would make leaving a little more bearable.
    "You two really did an amazing job!" Aunt Jane kept on saying proudly.

Arriving back at the house, Ann got the mail. A letter had arrived from her family back home. She knew she probably shouldn't bother with a reply since she would see them before the letter would get to them.

The letter read as follows:

Dear Ann,

We hope the competition goes very well! We are looking forward to seeing you! We heard about the fire there and are glad you are safe. Your Aunt Jane phoned me about it. Your father has accepted a new job opportunity near your cousins. Meaning you will have a second home! We will be living in the yellow farmhouse. Danny says hello. See you soon!

    We love you!

     Mom & Dad

Ann ran to tell Dick that they would be neighbors; it was so exciting!

"You're joking!" Dick was more excited than ever.

Ann smiled. She could just begin to imagine what fun they would have with a neighbor like Dick… you were just destined to.

"By the way, what happened when you first started riding?" asked Ann, changing the subject. The mysterious past was still on her mind.

Chapter Nineteen: The Secret

Dick looked kind of embarrassed. "Oh, I guess I can tell you. Well, I *was* younger then. Mom and Dad wanted me to learn how to ride, but they thought it would be better for me to take some classes. I got on a horse for the first time but uh... the horse just wouldn't move. I tried real hard, and yet the whole time I was there, he didn't move at all. The instructors kept telling me I was doing this and that wrong, but I thought there was just something wrong with the horse. All the other horses were being ridden though, so... I guess that is pretty much the whole story."

"Oh," was all Ann said. She felt rather bad she'd pried. Her curiosity was getting the better of her.

"Anyway," Dick changed the subject, "it's going to be great! I mean, that is, you living so close."

"Yeah, it will be great!" Ann agreed excitedly. She still could hardly believe she was going to live so close. It was such a surprise! And she could come and ride her favorite horse, Autumn, frequently. Ann wondered if when fall came she would go to school with Dick. *I suppose he would be in an older grade than me,* thought Ann. It really didn't matter. It was just going to be so fun!

Dinner was macaroni and cheese, it was homemade by Pam, and Aunt Jane made some buttery biscuits to go with. It was absolutely delicious. Afterwards, Ann went outside. She took Clover out and played with her in the temporary pen Uncle Nick had made. She wouldn't really have to move at all, not very far anyways. She supposed her aunt and uncle had to have known about this since they were letting Ann's family have the farmhouse. She wondered how they could keep such a secret. Ann bent down on her knees and stroked Clover's fur. She was such a calm rabbit.

The sun set low in the sky. The pink and purple shades died away. Ann put Clover back into her cage. Returning to the house, a magnificent smell filled the air. Ann hurried to the kitchen. Dick's grandma was just taking a raspberry pie out of the oven. "Hello, Ann. Just testing my cooking skills. The rest of the family is in the living room."

"Well, I remembered that I wanted to ask you something. That yellow farmhouse we are moving into, it was one of your husband's property before. In a shed nearby, there's a few photos and things in there of yours and your husband's. Perhaps you would like them?"

"Oh," said Grandma Margaret. "I did forget about those. I forget so many things these days. It would be nice to have them. Henry was so dear to me. Thank you."

Ann left to go to the living room, and Grandma soon joined them. "Oh, Ann," she said. "Remind me to get the pictures, and we can check out the farmhouse after church tomorrow. I haven't been there in a long time."

"That should be great."

Soon it was bedtime, Ann kissed Grandma and Aunt Jane goodnight.

The following afternoon, after church and lunch, Ann reminded Grandma Margaret of going to get the photos. "Oh yes," said Grandma, "I almost forgot." Off they set with a snack of crackers and cheese in a basket just in case they got hungry. It was a beautiful day out in the woods. The dark green of the forest was quiet and cool. They breathed in the sweet scented air. Chattering chipmunks gathered clusters of pine cones and assortments of seeds in their chubby cheeks. Birds twittered here and there. A red squirrel raced across the path.

Ann saw a dark brown bunny hop into the trees.

"Look there on the cliff!" Dick whispered energetically. Ann turned to see that in the trees on the cliff there was a doe and her fawn hurrying off. God's beautiful nature was abundant in these woods.

The walk to the farmhouse was a rather long one, but after some time they reached it. "First we should get the photos," Grandma Margaret suggested wisely. Inside the neat little shed, Ann showed Grandma the pictures inside a drawer of a little wooden desk. "Oh these," the elderly woman recalled, "I happen to be the photographer."

"Really?" asked Dick, "It must have been exciting to be there with him."

"Oh, yes, it certainly was just that." She put the things into her purse and they exited the shed.

The farmhouse was charming but small. The roof was an ivory green and it had a little brick chimney. In the inside they first entered into the living room. It was bare except a few odds and ends. They continued into the dining room. It had a polished wood floor and very fancy hanging lights.

"I used to love this little house," Grandma Margaret murmured, with a faraway look in her eyes.

"Why did you leave?" Ann wondered aloud.

"It reminded me too much of Henry, bless his soul."

"Does it make you sad to be here now?" Ann asked tenderly, always touched by another's emotional feelings.

"No, I am happy to see it once more. You're going to have wonderful times, child."

"I'm sure I will."

Ann explored the house which would be her home in a matter of days. There was a very attractive room that was Grandma's old bedroom. The window had a good view outside. The walls were painted a pale pink and... "What is this?!" Ann suddenly exclaimed.

Grandma and Dick came in. Ann bent over a little door in the floor. She had kicked into a small loop of metal that looked like it came up as a handle. The door was very small, about one foot by two feet. Dick looked questionably at his grandmother. "Should we open it?"

"No!" Grandma sounded a little too firm. "I mean, it might be dangerous." She said this in a softer tone.

"Come on... what could be so dangerous?" Dick asked.

"Just things."

"Well I'm going to find out what 'things' are. I don't want anything dangerous in Ann's house," Dick said. Grandma Margaret wanted to protest but could find nothing to say.

Dick opened the somewhat sticky door. It squeaked as the hinges were being moved. Inside was a small well worn dark box. Dick opened it and lifted out a little blue book. In gold glitter read the words: *Dear Diary*. Dick opened it. "Why, this is your diary, Grandma!"

Grandma Margaret snatched it from his hands. "It's just a bit of nonsense."

"But can't we read it?" Dick asked.

"I'd like to know more about you," Ann put in.

"It was a while back," Grandma Margaret began. "Only when Dick was a few months old. We were still living here. It just tells of different things me and your Grandpa did. About some of his crazy adventures."

"That sounds exciting." Dick was very eager.

"Oh, alright. I suppose you can read it if you'd really like. I hid it long ago. It's kind of embarrassing." Grandma handed the book to Dick.

Ann and him began to read the entries. They were very intrigued as they read of the lots of exciting horses her husband had tamed from the wild or rescued. It even included the finding of Autumn when she was abandoned as a baby. The story was in full detail. And there *was* some mention of a gray and white pony named June. So that's what Grandma had been talking about!

"Henry brought home a cute little gray and white pony. He is gentle and stalky. Henry's friend could not care for him because of expenses on his bad hooves that require special medication. But Henry knew we could make by and help June. I rather fancy him. I made him some of my favorite horse treats, he loves those! I hope we can keep him, he'd be a shame to lose…" Dick and Ann read on.

"Children!" Grandma Margaret interrupted, "You can take that book home for all I care! But we really should be getting back."

"Silly us!" said Dick. "I'm sorry to have kept you waiting… it's just that, you see, it's so interesting!"

"Oh never mind!" Grandma tossed the compliment aside, although Ann could tell she was blushing. They started back through the woods munching on their snack.

When they came home, Pam asked Ann, "How about doing some more of that patch work quilt we were working on before?"

119

"Sure." Ann did kind of want to read more of the diary, but maybe she should do something with Pam. She was always with Dick.

The girls set up the sewing machine and set to work. It was while Pam was cutting more squares that Ann noticed something on Pam's hand. On her fourth finger she saw a silver ring with a diamond. Ann had never seen Pam where it before. Pam was eighteen, could she be engaged? Pam must have caught Ann looking at it for she pulled her hand underneath the table.

Ann wanted to ask Pam about it. But would she seem rude to pry? Ann opened her mouth to speak…

Chapter Twenty: Blueberry Ridge Memories

"Pam, ah… do you mind if I ask you about it?"

"What?" Pam asked, although Ann felt she *had* to know.

Ann said bluntly, "Are you getting married?" Then feeling rather awkward at the silent response, Ann said, "I'm sorry, I didn't mean to upset you or pry, it's just that…"

Pam cut her short, "It's okay. I would tell you soon enough anyway. I am engaged to a man named Michael Sargent." Pam blushed as she said his name.

"That's wonderful!" Ann hugged her older cousin. Her cousin seemed even more grown up now, and Ann felt a little shy.

The two then continued to sew the quilt. It was coming along very nicely. Ann fed the cloth through the machine and pressed her foot down on the pedal. The needle went up and down poking through the squares of material. Pam was an excellent teacher, and, Ann thought, would probably make an excellent wife.

Dick walked in from the doorway with Grandma Margaret's diary in his hand. He read as he walked. Suddenly his face lit up with excitement. He pressed a hurried hand on Ann's shoulder. "Look, here! This is funny!" he cried, bursting with laughter. Ann abruptly stopped the sewing machine and turned her head to Dick.

"What is it?"

"Right here. Just read this page. This is cool."

"Okay, it'll be just a minute Pam," Ann took the small book from her excited cousin. Dick pointed to the page. It read as follows:

"Today was one of the most interesting days of my *life*. Henry was out in the barn and I was watering the tulips in the backyard next to the porch. Well, I don't know what exactly happened, I'm still so confused. I think Henry called me to the barn. I came, dropping my watering can in the grass. I hurried inside. Henry said to me, 'See here this little pony? He's doing just fine. I think it's about time you ride him.' I couldn't believe my ears! Me? Ride? I'd never ridden a horse or a pony for that matter, in all the years of my life!"

Here Ann stopped and looked up at Dick. "What!? She never rode before?" Ann was shocked!

"Yeah, she's just like you, but keep reading. It gets exciting."

"Okay," Ann smiled at Dick.

She read on:

"I stood there dumbfounded. Henry, he got June all saddled up and the reins on. June is a stocky thing and has strong legs, but I was scared to death. It seems funny now. Me being only a few feet off the ground! June is only thirteen hands tall afterall. Somehow or other I managed to get on. Squeezing the reins till my fingers were white, I was all tense. Henry told me to relax, but of course I couldn't. Then the pony walked and trotted while Henry guided him. And then, as if that wasn't scary enough, Henry told me he was going to let go. The next moment I knew was that June was galloping away and it felt like I was flying. Until... Splat!! I was covered in mud on the ground. Later, I learned that apparently June had seen an especially green and yummy clump of grass to eat and raced over to it. I, having never ridden before and having been told to relax, let go of everything; and so June ran forward and since I wasn't holding on, I was left behind in a muddy puddle left

122

over from the rain. I still laugh with tears in my eyes when I think of it."

Dick laughed as Ann finished. "See how good you are at riding?!" he exclaimed.

Ann broke into a smile. "That certainly was quite a story," she said, avoiding the compliment. Praise from Dick made her feel a little nervous.

"I can hardly believe that tomorrow I'm moving," Ann was now speaking to both of her cousins.

"It was great having you," Dick spoke up.

"And we'll still have great times," Pam reminded them, "You won't be far away."

"Yeah, and we can meet your brother and the rest of your family," Dick chimed in.

Soon Ann and Pam were done sewing, and Dick thought they should all three go on a trail ride. Ann was happy to include Pam on their adventure. They all rode their favorite horses: Ann on Autumn; Dick on Black Mystery; and Pam on Lilac. "Ivy is going to be so jealous when he finds out you like Mystery more than him," Pam teased her younger brother.

"I do not! I like them both," Dick protested, "I would ride Ivy, it's just that I can't."

"Yeah, I know, I was just teasing."

Lilac led the way, Black Mystery following, and Autumn bringing up the rear. They rode single file for a ways until the trail widened. The day was cool and breezy. Ann felt peaceful and happy. Her soft brown hair blew in the breeze. The scenery was beautiful and the air was sweet.

No one said much, but it didn't seem awkward at all. It was just great to be in the woods riding horses with friends. They rode for a long time until they came to Crystal Lake, that was what Ann and Dick had named the lake where they had seen Mystery on the other side.

The water was clear and sparkling as usual. There were many smooth pebbles on the sandy bottom. "It would be great to go swimming here sometime," said Dick.

"Yeah," Ann agreed.

The three cousins traveled back. Nearing the house they saw a strange car parked in the driveway; except Ann recognized it. "Why, it's Mom and Dad!" she cried.

"I thought they were coming tomorrow?!" Pam was surprised.

The front car door opened and Ann's mother stepped out. It had been so long! "Mom! Look! I'm over here!" Ann called.

"My! Look at you!" Ann's mother exclaimed as she approached the riders.

The cousins slid off their horses at the wooden steps. Ann's father came over as well. "Where's Danny?" Ann asked as the hugged her parents.

"Surprise!" Danny shouted, pouncing on his sister from behind.

Ann screamed in surprise. "You little trickster!" Ann hugged her mischievous brother. His dark eyes sparkled. His short dark brown hair and his smiling mouth were very familiar. Danny was almost eight years old.

"How come you came early?" Ann asked.

"We wanted to surprise you," said her father.

"I'm so glad you've come. It's been so fun here and I know I'll love my new home," Ann told them excitedly.

"I'm sure you will," Ann's mom agreed, adding, "the moving truck will be coming tomorrow."

"I want to see the horses!" Danny pleaded impatiently, all the talk was boring him.

"I'll show you," said Ann, "Coming, Dick?"

"Sure. They need to be groomed from our ride, anyhow."

Dick and Ann groomed the horses from their ride, while Danny "watched." All he really did was dance around and ask questions while getting in their way.

"Alright, time to go in," said Dick when they were finished and had put the horses in the barn.

"I think it's dinner time," said Danny.

"How do you know?" asked Dick.

"I'm hungry, so it's dinner time," was the prompt reply.

Ann smiled at her silly little brother.

But Danny proved to be right. Sure enough, dinner was ready. They ate lasagna and garlic bread. It was delicious and buttery. As they cleared the table Danny asked, "Where are we sleeping tonight?"

"Well, there aren't any beds at the farmhouse yet, so you can sleep in the guest room," Aunt Jane told him pleasantly.

"Can I see the room?"

"Danny don't be rude," Mrs. Melonwood reminded her impatient son.

"I'll show him," Grandma Margaret readily offered, unaware of the burden she had just put on herself.

Grandma Margaret led the little boy down the hallway. They passed rooms mysterious to curious Danny, all of them looking intriguing, but it was not for a long ways till at last Grandma said, "Here it is." She opened the large wooden door. There was a cobwebbed staircase leading into a dark room.

"Oops!" Grandma cried, "This is not the correct one. Sorry, Danny, I must have forgotten quite where the guest room is."

"But it looks cool, can't we go down?" asked the always-curious boy.

"I don't think that would be a wise decision."

"Why not?"

"Because," Grandma sighed, growing tired of his rapid questions and curiosity, "Well... I'm not sure where it leads and..."

Danny was already running down the steep steps, not waiting for another word.

"Stop! Be careful! Don't run!" Grandma Margaret cried in a jumble of emotions.

"Come on," a little voice said, "It's real cool down here."

"Oh, very well," Grandma reluctantly followed Danny down. It was almost pitch black as she nervously felt the wall until she could find some sort of light.

At last, she found one and switched it on quickly. A dim light flickered about the room. Grandma could not see Danny anywhere. "Danny, where are you?" she questioned timidly.

"You'll have to find me!" a voice squeaked in response. Grandma glanced around for him, noticing that the room was definitely a basement filled with many tools, some of them very dangerous.

"Danny, this isn't funny!" She shrieked.

"You're getting close..." a voice echoed around the spacious room.

Grandma peered over a plastic box.

"Boo!"

"Ah!" Grandma exclaimed in surprise.

"Scared you!" Danny cried gleefully.

"Children these days," Grandma sighed, "always getting on my poor nerves. Now, you just come with me, young man." Grandma firmly grasped his arm and pulled him back upstairs. She led him down the hallway to a different room, a few doors away. "Here is the right one," she said, "sorry for the confusion, but as you get on in years, you'll understand that it's quite easy to forget quite where things are. Just don't run off again…"

But Danny wasn't really listening, he was too busy exploring his temporary bedroom.

Meanwhile, the rest of the family had finished cleaning up and were playing a card game. So far, Dick seemed to be having all the luck. That is, until Grandma and Danny came back, and Grandma Margaret proved herself to be ten times as lucky as Dick.

"It's time for bed," yawned Aunt Jane, as they finished the round.

"Already?" Ann asked while glancing at the clock which confirmed her Aunt's statement. She had been having so much fun she hadn't realized it was already ten o'clock! They packed up their game and headed to the living room to say their night time prayer. Uncle Nick began and they all followed his lead, their voices filling the room in chorus. As they finished, Ann silently added a prayer of her own:

Thank you, God, for this wonderful time at Blueberry Ridge. Thank You for my aunt and uncle, my cousins, and my family. You have been so good to me. Thank You for this wonderful time at Blueberry Ridge. Thank you, thank you, thank you!

About the Authors

Gloria, Grace, and Virginia have written several novels together, all available from Talley Publishing (www.talleypublishing.com). *At Blueberry Ridge* is their second published novel, and a sequel, *Neighbors with Blueberry Ridge*, will be available soon.

Gloria, Grace, and Virginia live in Michigan and Wisconsin. They enjoy knitting, crocheting, music, arts and crafts, reading, and pet bunnies.